HER SOLID GROUND

HER SOLID GROUND

SHAMEKA S ERBY

Dedication

To everyone finding their way home.

Content Warning

Violence and a smidge of death, parental neglect and abuse, mentions of human trafficking and captivity, and a slight lactation kink. Maybe breeding too.

ISBN-13: 9798990426528
Cover design by: The Chary Assist
Edits By: AK Edits
Printed in the United States of America

Prologue

Elliott "Easy" Tanner hopped out of the car and headed up to his front door. He disarmed the house from his phone and threw a one-handed wave up to Dave, the worker who dropped him off. His car was in the shop again, something with the alternator this time. Keona kept bugging him to get a new one, but the car had sentimental value; it was the only thing his father ever gave him. But his dad was gone. Maybe it was the car's time to go too. For my birthday, I'll let Key pick out my new whip, he thought. Then maybe he could convince her to get an upgrade too. She insisted her car was still good, but she was overdue for something better. And it wasn't like they couldn't afford it.

He shut the front door behind him, knowing it would lock automatically, and headed up the stairs to the living room. Everything was quiet on this level, but he heard noises upstairs like Keona was moving things around. Easy shook his head. She was probably reorganizing their closet or something. He headed up, smiling as he thought of his baby. Maybe he could convince her to take a break so he could bend her thick ass over real fast.

When he entered the bedroom, the first thing he registered was an open duffle bag on their bed. Then he heard bumping and sniffling coming from their walk-in closet. A second later, Keona walked out with her arms full of clothes. Her caramel eyes were red-rimmed like she'd been crying; he could see the tear tracks drying on her cheeks. Her brown skin was splotchy, and she looked flushed and very obviously upset.

"I... I was leaving you a note," she offered, her voice barely more than a whisper. Easy blinked, and he got a sick feeling in the pit of his stomach.

"Are you...going somewhere?" he asked quietly. Keona nodded.

"I, um… I can't—look, this isn't working out, okay?" she said, moving to the bed. She dumped the clothes in her arms into the duffle bag and stood there, hands shaking, refusing to look at him. Easy took a deep breath, wanting to control his response.

"Keona, tell me what's happening here? Is something wrong? Did I do something?"

"You're just—this is not what I want anymore, okay? I'm leaving."

"Leaving what? Leaving me? Leaving our house? No, you not. What are you talking about?" Easy said back, his confusion making way for frustration. Why wouldn't she look at him?

"You don't own me, Elliott. I can go anywhere I want, and I'm going away from here. From you. I need space and—"

"If you need space, we can move all the furniture out of this muthafucka. Because you ain't going nowhere. Keona, look at me. Look at me and talk to me. What's happening right now?" he demanded. Keona shook her head and rubbed her face with her hand hurriedly, like she didn't want him to see her tears. But it was too late.

"This is not meant to be, Elliott. I-I'm…better than this. It's time to move on to someone who can give me what I deserve," she insisted, trying to sound serious. Easy snorted. Move on? A joke at best and a dangerous promise at worst.

"I can tell when you lying, and you need to tell me the truth, right now. Cause the only thing your ass gon deserve is a dead man on your conscience if I find out another nigga even **thought** about touching you. Don't play with me, Key."

"Why can't you accept that I don't want you anymore?" she said, her voice rising.

"Maybe I could if you looked me in the eyes when you fucking said it," he shot back.

"Stop making this hard. I am leaving, and I don't owe you an explanation," Keona said, turning and escaping into the closet again.

Easy clenched his fists and closed his eyes, counting to ten, then twenty. He fought to keep his feet still, keep from running up in the closet and physically restraining her. He'd never touched Keona with anything but love in his hands and he wouldn't start now.

She came out again with an armful of her things and threw them into the duffle bag. Her hands were shaking again, and when her eyes flicked to his for a second, he saw fear. And he panicked. Because experience had taught him he'd be the last person to know if his girlfriend was afraid of something. It was an ever-present frustration in their otherwise perfect relationship.

"Tell me what you're afraid of. I promise I'll fix it, Key. Please don't run out of here without giving me a chance to fix it," he begged her. She sighed and shook her head.

"I'm not afraid of anything. I decided it was time to move on, that's all. This was a nice little interlude. But my life is meant to be more than this."

"More than what?"

"More than shacking up with a middle management nigga. I want to be the head bitch. I'll never get there if—"

"You ain't never wanted that in your fucking life. And didn't I tell you to stop lying to me?"

"Elliott, you're not good enough, okay! You never have been, you never will be!" she yelled, going back into the closet again.

Easy caught his breath, feeling like she'd punched him in the chest. His common sense told him Key was only trying to hurt him, to push him away on purpose. But he couldn't stop the effect of her words on his heart.

"Key, I'm asking you not to do this," he said, his voice strained. Keona came out of the closet, still not looking at him, throwing more clothes in the bag.

"I have to want better for myself; you're not going to give it to me. I'm tired of being stuck here while you play third to Romelo and Trevino. You haven't even tried to build something of your own. You can stay here and be satisfied with whatever they hand you. I'm going to find a real man," she said, zipping the bag. She brushed past him and left the room, still refusing to look him in the eye, and Easy knew she was full of shit. No argument of theirs had ever escalated so quickly, and Keona didn't say mean things for sport. Something was chasing her out of here, and he had to find out what it was.

He followed her down the stairs. "Keona Ross, don't walk out of this fucking house."

"Or what? You don't own me, nigga!" she spat out, finally turning to face him. Her plush body was vibrating with anger, but those eyes were telling on her. She was scared as hell. Easy took another deep breath, trying to rein in his emotions and not let her words get to him.

"I'm going to ask you one more time to tell me what's going on," he said, his frustration making his voice hard. Keona rolled her eyes and threw her free hand on her hip.

"There's nothing going on. I'm just...over this. Over you, this relationship, and this so-called good life. I know there's better out there, and you can't compare, so don't even bother competing," she said, neck rolling as she looked him up and down. Easy shook his head, let out a low growl. Fine. If she wanted to play this fucking game, she could win the prize.

"Fuck it. I ain't never had to beg nobody to stay and I ain't starting with you. Fuck outta here, Key. I hope you outrun whoever has you so scared you losing your mind, talking to me like this. And I hope he can carry your ass 'cause I'm finished."

"I hope you mean it. I'm serious, Elliott. Stay away from me."

"You ain't gotta worry about it, ma. We done," he spat out and went back upstairs. Moments later, the garage opened and her old Volkswagen pulled away. Easy fell onto his bed, pain and anger warring for space in his chest. He had no idea what just happened and no idea what to do next.

1

Chapter One

*K***eona**
Two Years Later

Keona Mikayla Ross slung her tote bag over her shoulder and carried three packed duffle bags out to her car, the old Volkswagen she'd first arrived in. She was hardly allowed to go anywhere and was driven when she did, so no one would be looking for this car. It was a bit of a surprise the Wolf, aka her father, hadn't gotten rid of it. Since she'd hidden a spare key in the fabric of one of her jackets, keeping the car was certainly a mistake on his part. Oh, well, his bad. By the time he realized said mistake, she'd be long gone.

Once everything was loaded, she went back into the house, looking around one last time. Then she went into the library, pulled a book by the spine, and watched the wall shift away. Her father's safe came into view. Keona put in the combination, swinging the door open and peering in. The safe had a few stacks of cash and a small jewelry box; the rest was paperwork and bonds. Keona grabbed one of the stacks of cash and the box, opening it and removing a gold locket. Elliott had given it to her, and it was the first thing her father took away. He'd kept it to remind her of his threats whenever she dared get out of line.

Satisfied she wasn't taking anything that could be used to track her, she went to her bedroom to get the one thing she couldn't leave behind. Leaning over the bed, she scooped up her sleeping child, kissing his face and rocking him gently. The baby fussed a little and settled down again, drooling against her shoulder.

"Time to go, Lil Man," she whispered in his ear, grabbing his favorite stuffed animal and his blanket. "Time to go see Dada."

Keona left the house and put her son in his car seat. She hopped into the driver's seat and started the car, looking back at the luxury prison she was leaving behind. It was a quick look because the security camera reboot would be finished soon, and everything would be working again. She turned on the radio, letting the low instrumental music play a soundtrack to her thoughts. She'd make her first stop in a couple of hours, to change her son, get them both some breakfast, and see if she could find a prepaid cell phone. Keona sighed. She had to use her time wisely. Her father wouldn't be home from his trip for another week at least, which meant she had a week to get to Elliott, tell him about their son, and convince him to keep EJ safe while she got further away. The thought of leaving her sweet baby gave Keona pains in her chest, but his father was the only one she could trust. She didn't expect Elliott to protect her too, not after the way she'd left him, and not with her suddenly reappearing with the son he never knew about. If he took their child, it would be enough for her. She'd manage the rest on her own.

Two hours later, Keona pulled into a rest stop. Her son, Elliott Joseph Tanner III, or "EJ," was awake and whining, ready for milk. Keona parked at the far end of the lot for privacy, then got into the backseat with her baby, took him out of the chair, and lifted her shirt, cradling him as she popped a breast into his mouth. EJ sucked greedily, his eyes closing and his little jaws working. Keona sat back against the seat, sighing deeply. She'd been trying to wean him gently, but now there was no help for it. She would have to pump as much as she could before she left and hope EJ adapted quickly. Two tears fell down her cheeks and Keona swallowed, trying to stay under control. Tears wouldn't help her now. Once EJ was safe with his father and she was far away, then she would cry.

Keona left the rest stop after using the bathroom to freshen her and EJ, getting them both an egg sandwich, and buying some essentials, including some readymade food, spring water, a prepaid cell phone, and some snacks. Hours passed, and finally, Keona pulled into a motel in her hometown. She used cash to rent a room for three nights; she figured it was enough time to convince Elliott to keep their son. Once she was in the room, she took a quick shower while EJ slept, fed him half a sandwich and nursed him, then played with him and his shape toys until he fell asleep again. Keona got into bed beside her son, holding him close. She thought of his father, her only love, the man she'd most likely made an enemy by walking out on him without an explanation and disappearing with no contact. Keona sighed.

She hadn't accepted things being over with her and Elliott; she always hoped one day he'd be able to forgive her. But this wasn't the time or the situation to ask it of him. It was too much, and their family deserved better. They deserved a real chance to try, not a rush to forgiveness because she was in trouble. Keona didn't bother wiping the tears falling onto her cheeks this time. She missed her man and was about to miss her baby. Maybe it was time to cry after all.

The next day, Keona got dressed and had breakfast quietly. She didn't need noise anyway; her thoughts were blaring and intrusive, like a TV when you've lost the remote. EJ woke soon after her and she fed him some cereal, played with him, and talked to him about going to ask his daddy for help. EJ didn't understand, of course, but Keona never missed a chance to tell him how much trust she had in Dada. If only she'd been able to tell Elliott.

After, she gave him a small dose of cough syrup and nursed him into his mid-morning nap. He was getting over a little cold, but the syrup was mostly so he'd sleep a little longer. She left the room, locking it behind her, and got into her car. Keona had a sick feeling in the pit of her stomach, leaving EJ alone. But there was nowhere to take him. Hopefully, she wouldn't be too long.

When she pulled up in front of Elliott's three-story townhouse, memories flooded back with a vengeance, twisting up her stomach even more. Keona chose this house with him. She'd decorated, picked out their furniture, and made love to Elliott in every single room to welcome them home the first night. This was *her* house too. She took a deep breath, trying to get her stomach and bowels under control.

"Do it, Key," she whispered to herself. "It's not for you, it's for EJ. Get out of the damn car."

After another deep breath, she opened the door, exiting the vehicle. She hurried to Elliott's front door, not giving herself time to get nervous. Keona pushed the doorbell once, twice, her fingers shaking. After a moment, she could hear someone coming down the stairs. The first level was simply the garage and a small storage space behind it—there was nothing beyond the front door but a small entryway with the stairs to the upper level and another door on the side leading to the garage. Keona heard a surprised gasp, then the click of the locks before the door was yanked open.

"What the hell are *you* doing back here?" Laney Childs, once her longtime friend and confidant, looked at Keona with an angry sneer. Keona was surprised but fixed her face to mask it...and the hurt. What the hell was she expecting? For Elliott not to move on? She was disappointed it was with someone she'd thought of as her friend but reasoned that the two of them probably bonded through their shared anger. After all, she'd left Laney without a word too.

"Laney? I didn't know—never mind. Look, I need to speak to Elliott. Can you ask him to come down?"

"*Easy* doesn't want to talk to you, and neither does anyone else. Go back to wherever you came from, Key. It's too late."

"I know you're upset with me, and you have a right to be, but—"

"I'm not upset, baby girl. You showed me what you thought of our friendship and I'm matching your energy. As for Easy, he's very well taken care of, so like I said, you can go," Laney spat out, her frown deepening.

Keona took a deep breath, tried to be calm. But the old Keona was brimming under the surface, the one who swung first and talked later. The one who didn't let anyone give her shit or question her place, especially where Elliott was concerned. She balled her fists, counting to ten. *This is for EJ,* she reminded herself. She could take it—for EJ.

"You can hate me later, Laney. This is an emergency. I need to see Elliott, right now," she insisted. Laney sucked her teeth and propped one hand on her hip.

"And I said he don't want to see you."

"Okay, I don't have time for this. I can apologize as much as you want later, but you need to move before I move you. You know I don't have a problem throwing hands, Laney. And you know I don't play about my man."

"*Your* man? Bitch—"

"Yo, Laney, what the fuck? I told you to let whoever it was in on your way out, not argue in my fucking doorway. Why— Keona?" Amid their push and pull, the owner of the house jogged down the stairs, stopping short when he looked into her eyes.

Elliott Joseph Tanner II. Her love. The man who was once her life. The streets called him Easy, but she never had; she left his nickname for his friends, his work associates, for the women who wished he'd been as deep in their guts as he was in hers while they were together. She left his nickname for the people who couldn't see inside his heart, who couldn't read his soul. To her, he was Elliott—always had been, always would be.

He looked the same, his six foot two frame towering over her five foot six one with ease. Elliott was slender, his body unassuming, but he was strong, and his muscles were defined; he'd lifted her thick ass many a night in their bedroom. His skin was the color of hickory, a shade past syrup, almost carob but not quite. And his eyes were huge—big and round, almond-colored and always open. That's why they called Elliott "The Watcher." He was the most observant person she knew, and his eyes never missed a lie. Keona was counting on his discernment. It was how he would know she was telling the truth about EJ. Those eyes went into a beautiful wide nose and full mouth, and Keona was in love as she looked at him again and again. Her heart never wavered for this man. But now, his full mouth was twisted in a scowl as he waited for her to speak. She swallowed nervously.

"Yes, it's me. Hi, Elliott. I'm sorry to come here like this, but we have to talk. I need your help."

"My he—my help? After two years, that's what you have to say to me? You only here because you need something from me?" he yelled. He moved closer, outside now, and Keona backed away from his anger, wondering if she'd made a mistake. *Maybe I hurt him too badly,* she thought.

"Exactly. Coming back here, slumming because you want a favor—"

"I told you I don't play about my man, Laney. Mind your fucking business!" Keona exploded, turning to her ex-friend. Confronting Elliott might make her nervous, but confronting another bitch *about* him was never an issue. She turned back in time to see a ghost of a smile on his face. He remembered how she got down. Keona's spirits lifted. Maybe she hadn't ruined everything after all. Laney stood there in shock, anger coming off her in waves.

"Easy, are you gonna stand here and let her—"

"Honestly, this is a lot in front of my door, and I think both of y'all need to go," he said, sighing deeply. Keona clasped her hands together, getting desperate. She had to make him understand.

"You're sending me away? She's the one who doesn't belong here," Laney said.

"Elliott, please. I need five minutes. I have to talk to you. It's an emergency," Keona begged, unashamed. She was past her pride. This was about EJ.

"Laney, you don't belong here either. You told me what you came to tell me, now leave. Keona, I don't know what you want, but the answer is no," Easy said, sounding tired and sad. Laney stomped off to her car, but Keona remained, her eyes wet and stinging. They stared at each other for a long moment. Then he turned to go back inside.

"Elliott, baby, please—"

"Key, stop it, goddammit. I don't care what you need—"

"I need you to take care of our son!" she called to his back.

Elliott stopped. He turned, his big eyes on her...staring into her soul.

Elliott

Elliott Joseph "Easy" Tanner considered himself a levelheaded man. Controlled and calm, unmoved by dramatic displays and extraneous emotions. But Keona's words started a fire in his chest. He wanted to scream, cry, rage, hit something. He had a son. Keona had given birth to his baby. Where was his son? Why did she need him to take care of him? And if she hadn't suddenly "needed" him, would he ever have known?

"What did you say?" he asked.

Keona stood her ground, though he could tell she was scared. She licked her plump lips and lifted her chin. He looked at her, seeing the truth in her eyes, and his heart stuttered. He was a father. He had a son. And his long-lost love, this beautiful, infuriating woman standing in front of him, was his mother.

"Our son needs your help, Elliott. I didn't have anywhere else to go. I don't have a lot of time—"

"Make time, Key," he growled, grabbing her by the arm and pulling her inside. He thrust her up the stairs while he shut and locked the door. Keona went up to the second level and stood in the middle of the living room, staring at the furniture like she didn't choose it and everything else in the house. Easy wanted to show his fury, but he knew he had to be patient with his ex-girlfriend. *And baby mama*, he thought bitterly. He closed his eyes, tried to control his breathing, tried to get a handle on his hurt and anger. But it was impossible. He had a child in the world. A baby boy he didn't know, who didn't know him.

"You were pregnant when you left me? You walked out this fucking door with my baby inside you?" he yelled, clenching his fists in frustration. Keona started to cry, wringing her hands and pacing.

"Elliott, I didn't know! I swear I didn't!"

"What the fuck happened when you found out, Key? Why you keep my son from me?"

"I didn't want to! I couldn't tell you! He wouldn't let me!"

"Who wouldn't let you? Who, Keona?"

She turned away, holding her head in her hands. Her shoulders were hunched, like the weight of the world was on them. Easy had the sudden urge to go to her, pull her close. He shook his head, stopping his ridiculous thoughts. She owed him every explanation in the world. Her comfort was the last thing he needed to worry about.

"I can't tell you," she finally whispered. "It's—it's complicated. But eight and a half months after I left you, I gave birth to our baby boy. I couldn't tell you then for the same reasons I couldn't tell you I had to leave—reasons I can't go into now—but he's yours, Elliott. Yours and mine. I'm trying to make things right. I have to go away, but there will be people coming after me, and I don't want EJ with me if they find me. I need you to keep him. He'll be safe with you." Keona explained in half-truths and cryptic clues, and Easy was more frustrated than when she'd first started talking.

"Who the fuck you running from, Key? You protecting some nigga? Is it the 'he' who wouldn't let you bring me my child?" Easy yelled, trying to speak softer but failing. Keona backed away from his anger and he stared at her. She'd flinched like he was going to hurt her. But she knew better. *His woman* knew better. What the hell had she been through?

"Elliott, please, it's not like you think—"

"Stop acting like you're afraid of me, Keona. I'm not him, who-ever the fuck he is. And if you came here to keep protecting him, you might as well give me my son and pack extra snacks for the road. Cause you gon need all your strength to mourn him when I find the nigga and he's taking a dirt nap."

"I'm sorry. I didn't mean for— I tried—" she stuttered, still crying.

Easy took a deep breath, knowing his energy was feeding her fear and she'd never give him a straight answer until she was settled. "Calm the fuck down. You're gonna make yourself sick. I don't want to upset you more, I just... I need more information than you're giving me, Keona. You can't drop something like this on me and not explain yourself."

"I can't explain more, and what's going on with me doesn't matter. Will you help our son or not, Elliott?"

"I'll protect our son with my life. You already know that; it's why you brought him here in the first place. But I'm getting the information I need at some point. You ain't calling no shots here, Key. You need *me*, remember?" Easy said, his head beginning to hurt. He didn't mean to come across like this. Whether he knew about him or not, his protection of his son was absolute and unequivocal. He didn't want to give Keona the impression she needed to beg him to do it. But staring into her caramel eyes again, he was filled with so many conflicting emotions, and like it or not, anger was the loudest one. Keona nodded, wiping her wet cheeks.

"Y-You're right, Elliott. I apologize. Maybe I shouldn't have come."

"Maybe what? Maybe you should have kept my son from me a little longer? Why you doing this, Key? Tell me what's really going on!"

"I... Baby, I—" she stumbled and stuttered, folding her hands together tightly. Easy growled, feeling like he was about to explode. Why was this woman so stubborn?

"You being your same stubborn ass self for no reason! It was a problem in our relationship, and apparently, it still is," Easy said, his anger making him admit more hurt than he'd intended. Keona walked toward him, her eyes tortured.

"What do you mean? What was a problem in our relationship?"

"You never fully trusted me," he bit out, his mouth sour with the memories. "When something was hurting you or making you afraid, I had to force it out of you. You never shared your pain with me. It was like you didn't trust me to handle my shit like a man. To solve it, to protect you. It probably explains why you left me, right? You were caught up in something and you didn't think I could shield you from it. So, you ran instead of trusting me."

"I was trying to protect you!" Keona yelled, tears streaming down her face.

"I don't need your protection, Keona! I needed your love, your trust! Your *faith*!"

Keona gasped and reached for him, her eyes filled with remorse. "Elliott...baby, I—"

"You know what, Key? Fuck it. It doesn't matter. Where's my son?" Easy cut her off and turned away from her tears, pushing down his insecurities. Their son needed him. If it was the only reason Keona was here, he'd have to take it as it was. He wasn't going to beg her to trust him, especially since she was on her way out the door again. Keona sniffled and choked back a sob, and Easy's heart squeezed in his chest. This woman abandoned him. She didn't deserve his arms, his comfort. But damn if he didn't want to give them to her.

"I rented a room at the motel; I left him there sleeping," Keona admitted in a small voice. Easy turned back to her, scowling.

"You left him alone, Key?"

She started crying again. "I didn't have a choice. I didn't want people to recognize me and see him. And I can't trust anyone—"

"Take me to him **now**," Easy said, grabbing his car keys. He took Keona's hand and pulled her back down the stairs and through the side door into the garage, then flipped the switch to lift the garage door.

"Go pull your car in here; we'll take mine. Hurry up," he ordered, and Keona rushed to obey him as Easy got into his brand-new black Lexus NX SUV. His birthday recently passed and he'd decided to treat himself. It was a luxury car but still lowkey enough to drive through the hood. He'd even purchased a hybrid model; his best friend Trevino kept insisting they be more considerate of the planet and shit. Keona's Volkswagen pulled in beside him, then she hopped out of the car and ran to his passenger seat. Easy pulled out onto his driveway, hit the switch in his car for the garage door to close again, and then headed to the motel.

On the short ride, Easy kept stealing glances at his ex, whose mind seemed to be somewhere else. Her burnt umber skin was flushed because she was upset, and he could see all her red undertones. Her curly brown hair was pulled into a bun atop her head. When they were together, she spent hours styling it, sometimes keeping the coils tight so it looked more like an afro, sometimes separating and combing them out so it was looser and wavy. She bit her bottom lip and scratched her small, wide nose, her mind still far away. It gave Easy time to look at her plush body, still thick as the oatmeal his MomMom made every morning and blooming everywhere. Motherhood had taken Keona from extra thick to beautifully plump, and Easy found himself admiring it...and wanting it again.

When they got to the motel, Keona ran ahead, anxious to see their baby boy and know he was okay. She fumbled with the door key, and he finally took it from her shaking hands, unlocking the door himself. They pushed into the room and shut the door behind them, and Easy heard his son cry. His gaze went to the bed. The little boy was pushing out of a small pile of blankets, rubbing his eyes and looking for familiarity. His hair was a thick, curly bush like his mother's, but those big almond-colored eyes were his. This was his son.

"I'm right here, sweetness, Mama's right here. I'm so sorry I left you alone. Mama's so sorry," Keona said, going to the bed and scooping the baby into her arms, crying softly. She ran her hands over his little body, making sure he was uninjured, then hurriedly changed his diaper. Easy watched, speechless. His son was beautiful. His hickory skin was smooth and looked soft to the touch. He was a chunky boy, inheriting his mama's thickness along with her hair. Easy's hands shook; he wanted to hold him. The little boy whined and grabbed Keona's shirt. She lifted it without missing a beat, unhooking the front clasp of her bra and pushing a plump titty into their son's mouth, gently rocking him.

Elliott took a breath, his throat suddenly dry. He didn't know why the sight of his son nursing was causing such a visceral reaction. Maybe because her breasts had always been his favorite place to rest as well. Either way, his dick was getting hard, and his hands were tingling. Keona was beautiful as she nursed, slightly breathless, with her skin glowing, those red tones showing underneath. *She still takes my breath away,* Easy thought, and shook his head to clear it. No lovesick thoughts about Keona. She'd hurt and humiliated him. She was the mother of his child now and nothing else.

"You're still nursing?" he managed to ask, going to the other side of the room and sitting in a chair. Keona nodded as their son drank from her greedily, whimpering a little. Easy found himself wanting to whimper too, but for an entirely different reason.

"I've been trying to wean him," she said, smiling sheepishly. "As you can see, he's not having it."

"You said he was born eight months after you left. It means he's—"

"Almost a year and a half," Keona confirmed. Easy nodded. He got up from the chair, his nervous energy propelling him to the bed where he sat down next to her.

"What's his name, Key?" Easy whispered, reaching for one of the thick coils on top of his son's head. Keona stared at him, licked her bottom lip again, and took a breath.

"His name is...Elliott Joseph Tanner III. I call him EJ," she replied, whispering too. EJ finished drinking and let go of her nipple, pushing away from his mother's chest. Without thinking, Easy lifted the boy into his arms so Key could fix her clothes. He held him against his shoulder and patted his back. EJ burped loudly, and Easy smiled.

EJ pulled back and looked into his face, staring silently, his head tilted. Easy could feel his heart threatening to burst from his chest. This tiny human was his, and he loved him. Immediately. Irrevocably.

"You Dada," EJ cried out with a grin, as if he'd just figured it out. Easy's mouth dropped open. Then he smiled even bigger, his entire body humming.

"Yeah, baby boy," he said, "I'm Dada." EJ reached for him and held on tight. Easy looked over at Keona, who had tears running down her face.

"He called me—"

"I show him your picture every night, and I tell him about you. He knows you, Elliott. He was always gonna know you."

"Was I gonna know him, Key? If you weren't in whatever trouble you're in, if you didn't need me now, would I—"

"Yes, baby," she cut him off, walking over to them. "Everything got so complicated, and I made it worse. But I was going to make sure you knew him, I promise." She was still crying, and Elliott wanted to take her in his arms, kiss her hair. But they were past that now...weren't they? He sighed. There was so much hurt between them, so many things unsaid. He didn't know how to even begin to untangle it, but he knew they weren't going to do it in this dingy motel room. Plus, if someone really was on Keona's trail like she'd said, they might have already tracked her to this place. He had to take his family home.

"Where y'all stuff?" Elliott asked. Keona wiped her face and looked around.

"Most of it is in the car still. I was so tired when I got here last night, I didn't even bother with it."

"Grab whatever y'all got left. We getting out of here," Easy said, still holding onto his son. EJ lay against his shoulder, calm and quiet, watching. An observer, like his father. Easy smiled. Keona grabbed a baby blanket and a stuffed animal, plus some other things.

"I'm ready," she announced. They left the motel room, leaving the key inside. Keona took EJ in her arms and got into the backseat with him, cradling him where it was safer since they'd forgotten the car seat. Easy headed outside of town, going to a Target in a more suburban area and fortunately finding parking right up front.

"Come on. We gotta get him some stuff," was all he said before getting out. He went to the back door and opened it, reaching in for EJ so Keona could get out of the car.

"Why here?" she asked. Easy shrugged.

"I came a little further out because you're worried about people seeing you and knowing you're back in town," he replied and walked away with his son, leaving her to follow. He got a cart and put EJ in the front seat area. Keona caught up and nudged him aside, steering the cart. Easy went over to a sales associate and tapped him on the shoulder.

"My man. I'ma need one of those pushable dollies for some bulk items. I'm doing my son's room, and he needs everything."

"Of course, sir," the sales associate said and walked into customer service. Two minutes later, Easy and Keona were cruising up and down the aisles, the sales associate following with the dolly, getting a toddler bed, stroller, extra car seat, a toy chest, a Pack 'N Play, baby gates, and other things. Keona's cart was loaded with toys, bedding and pillows, a new breast pump, outlet covers, and everything Easy could think of. She tried to protest, but he shut her down every time. He was in charge now. EJ talked his baby talk, ate snacks from Keona's bag, clapped and laughed whenever something else hit the cart, and screamed "Dada!" every time Easy was in his line of sight. By the time they left the store, everyone was hungry.

"I can pick up something and we'll take it back to the house," Easy said to Keona. She was sitting beside him, their son secure in his new car seat behind her. She gave him a small smile.

"If you have groceries, I'll make you dinner," she offered instead. Easy shook his head. Cooking felt too much like settling in, and she'd already said she was leaving. He didn't need to get used to her being around.

"Key, you don't owe me—"

"Yes, I do," she interrupted. "I left you two years ago because I was scared and foolish, and I showed up here today the same way. I laid a lot on you, and it wasn't fair. I can at least cook you a meal while you spend some time with our son."

Easy nodded, letting her have her way. They got back to the house, and Keona took EJ inside to change him while Easy unloaded everything from his car and hers. He set up the baby gates to block the stairs and covered the electrical outlets. Keona fed EJ a mac and cheese cup, then spread a blanket in the middle of the living room and dumped toys onto it, sitting him among them. Then she went to the kitchen and opened the freezer and cabinets, looking for dinner ideas. The entire second level was open plan, so she could see EJ as she cooked. Easy went upstairs and started setting up EJ's bed in the empty room next to his and putting things away. He put Key's things in his bedroom closet and walked away before he could ask himself too many questions about why he'd done it. *What are you thinking? She's still trying to run away,* he told himself. *Her stubborn ass is lacing up her sneakers as we speak.*

Easy was still hurt and angry as hell, but he couldn't stop his heart from wanting Keona. And he couldn't help feeling like his family was right where they belonged.

Keona

Keona stirred her gravy slowly, careful not to let any lumps form. Smothered chicken with her special creamy mushroom gravy was Elliott's favorite and she wanted to get it right. She hadn't cooked in a long time; her father was more concerned with her losing weight and flaunting her alleged bedroom talents to his friends. Keona shivered when she thought of being sold off to one of them as a piece of property. It made her remember why she was here—and why she couldn't stay. Her father was an evil man who wouldn't be deterred easily. She refused to put Elliott in his crosshairs. One night, and then she'd say goodbye to her sweet baby and his wonderful father and be on her way. By the time her father realized she was missing, she'd have days on him. And hopefully, he'd never find her.

Keona turned the fire down low under her pan and picked up the plate of parcooked chicken thighs. One by one, she placed them back into the gravy and covered the pan with a lid. She started the rice and poured a bag of frozen broccoli into a bowl, sticking it in the microwave for when she was ready.

She looked over at her boys. EJ was sitting on his father's chest, laughing hysterically as Elliott made faces at him. Keona smiled, her heart bursting. This was how it should be. Maybe one day, when Elliott could forgive her and her father left her alone, maybe she could come back to her boys and be a family with them. Elliott was understandably angry with her, but he still paid attention to her fears about being seen and recognized, and he'd brought them home from the motel. Maybe forgiveness wasn't completely out of the question, especially if she was able to tell him what really happened. But for now, she had to take tonight and as many hours as she could tomorrow and hold it close to her heart. Keona finished dinner and made a small plate for EJ, mashing the soft, tender chicken together with the rice, gravy, and broccoli. Then she made a heaping plate for Elliott and a regular-sized one for herself.

"Come eat, you two," she called into the living room. Elliott stood up with their son and carried him into the eat-in kitchen. He settled EJ into a brand-new highchair and took his bib from her, securing it around their son's neck. Then he sat next to him, grabbing a spoon and scooping some of the mashed food.

"I can feed him, Elliott. Eat your dinner," she said, trying to take the spoon away. He dodged her hands and shook his head.

"You eat. Me and my boy are good. Thank you for the food. Can you tell Mama thank you, baby boy?" he said, directing the last part to their son. EJ grinned.

"Mama, dank you!" he yelled, and Keona laughed.

"You're welcome, baby. It's no problem. I hope it's still your favorite." She said the last sentences to Elliott. He nodded, smiling big.

"It is. MomMom makes it for me occasionally. I pretend like it hits the same as yours, but it doesn't," he admitted. Keona grinned, her face warm with pleasure. Elliott fed their son and helped him eat with his hands, talking softly to him, infinitely patient and calm. When EJ was nearly done, she grabbed Elliott's plate and warmed it so it would be piping hot again. Then she washed her own empty plate and grabbed their son from the highchair.

"I'll clean him up and get him ready for bed. You, eat your dinner," she said to her baby daddy and went upstairs. When she got to the room next to the master and saw the way everything was set up, she wanted to cry. This was the home EJ deserved. She gave her son a quick bath and dug through his bag for pajamas, then dressed and nursed him. By the time she was finished, Elliott was coming up the stairs.

"Key, that food was everything. Tastes as good as I remember. Why don't you take a shower, wind down? I'll read him a story," he said, coming into the room. Keona nodded and stood up, heading into the hall bathroom.

It wasn't lost on her that she and Elliott were still in their natural rhythm, moving seamlessly, like they lived together and coparented all the time. The realization only made her sadder. Her love had missed two years of watching their baby grow, both inside her body and out, but he still knew exactly what to do, exactly how to be a father. Elliott Tanner still knew how to love even though she'd broken his heart. Keona was confident her son would never know the fear and anguish she'd known with her own father, and she was grateful. But it broke her even more knowing she wouldn't be around to see it.

Her shower was long, the water as hot as she could stand, Keona using it to mask her tears. She had to leave her baby and his father, and the mere thought was twisting her stomach, piercing her chest. Keona finally washed and got out, wrapping herself in a huge bath sheet and going to find her clothes. The room with EJ's things was empty and she wandered into the master, curious as to where Elliott and EJ had gone.

She turned into the master bedroom and stopped, smiling. Elliott was sitting back against the headboard in fresh pajamas, dozing while EJ slept on his chest. The TV was playing a channel with ocean sounds and the lights were dim. Elliott started, opening his eyes. He went slack-jawed when he saw her in the towel, and Keona's body tingled from his hungry gaze.

"I-I was wondering where my clothes were," she asked softly. He pointed to his closet.

"I put them in with mine," he said. Keona went to the walk-in closet confused, but she wasn't about to ask questions. He'd laid some underwear and sleeping clothes out for her and lined the rest of her things up neatly on some empty shelves in the back. She stared, surprised and nervous. Did this mean Elliott wanted her to stay? But she couldn't...could she?

She hurriedly dressed, her mind racing through his rant about her not trusting him. Was he right? Did she simply need to ask for his protection? Keona shook her head, fluffing out her thick hair. This was too much for one day. She left the closet and went to the bed, intending to take EJ into his room and bunk next to him on the floor; she was almost positive Elliott didn't want her in their bed. She reached for EJ. Elliott moved her hand and patted the bed beside him.

"Come lay down, Key," he mumbled, his eyes still closed. Keona blinked; she was sure she must have heard wrong.

"Elliott, I can't— You don't have to—"

"I've been missing you beside me for two years. And I've never had my son with me. For one damn night, Keona, stop being so prideful and stubborn and give me this. Give me my family where they belong: next to me."

2

Chapter Two

*E*asy was up with the sun as usual, and he opened his eyes to find identical ones staring back at him. EJ grinned, reaching for him, and Easy pulled him close, untangling him from Keona's hold. He hugged his son to him, his chest getting tight with emotion. He was a father. The thought was still surreal, even though he and Keona always planned on having children.

Keona Ross moved to town at the beginning of their senior year in high school. Easy was on his way into street life, fast on the heels of his best friend Trevino, but knew he still wanted his diploma, at least. His immediate infatuation with the new girl became even more motivation for him to stay in school. They were fast friends and spent more time together than with anyone else. At the end of the school year, Keona asked him to take her to her senior prom, claiming she wouldn't have fun unless she was with him. The night of the prom, she gave him her virginity, and their relationship changed. But after a perfect summer, Keona went away to college, and they drifted apart. She stayed away four more years after graduating, content in her new life. Easy missed her, but they occasionally kept in touch, and ultimately, he was happy she was thriving.

On her twenty-sixth birthday, she came home. He was still in love, but he didn't want to pressure her and was fully ready to transition back into their friendship with no expectations for more. But Keona was ready for more. They burned hot and fast—their relationship was all gas, no brakes from the moment they reconnected. Easy thought his life was finally figured out. After six years of bliss, complete with a townhouse and plans to marry and have children, he came home one night, and Keona was packing. She said she wanted more than he could give, that his wants didn't match hers, that he was stifling her...holding her back. Easy didn't know where any of it was coming from, and he tried to question the look in her eyes, but she kept pushing him away, saying meaner and meaner things until he was so angry he agreed she should go. And two years later, she was back with his son.

He stared over at the mother of his child, his one and only love, and wondered how they'd gotten so far apart. His anger from the day before had abated some, leaving him with worry and a sickening confusion. Was there something he could have done to make Keona trust him with her troubles? Could he have stopped her two years ago? Should he have gone after her?

Questions swirled through his mind, frustrating him. Easy needed to spill out everything he was feeling, but the fear in Keona's eyes was stopping him. He still didn't know why she'd gone away, but he knew it was related to the reason she was back, and he knew whatever it was, she was genuinely afraid for EJ, which made Easy afraid for her. He couldn't let her walk away, not without the full story. But she was so set on leaving. How could he get her to stay?

EJ grabbed for his short beard, trying to grip the hairs, and re-captured his attention. Easy sat up with him, kissing him on the nose and rocking him. He felt his bottom and noticed the heaviness of his diaper.

"Let's get you changed and wiped down, baby boy," he said and eased out of bed, careful not to jostle Key or wake her. EJ was quiet as well, content to be in his arms. Easy got diapers, socks, and new pajamas from EJ's bag and then took the baby back into the master bathroom, letting him splash around the sink area while he brushed his teeth and washed his face. Then he wiped EJ down and changed him.

When EJ was in fresh pajamas and Easy was in sweats and a t-shirt, they went back to the bedroom area. Keona was still sleeping, hair out of her bonnet, drooling on the pillow. Easy frowned. She was weary, it was clear. He wondered again, as he had countless times since she left, what was going on with her, what burden she was trying to carry by herself. EJ whined a little and tried to jump out of his arms and go to Keona. Easy readjusted and held him tighter.

"Nah, son. You gon eat some soft eggs on toast and Dad's gonna find you some fruit. You getting old enough to leave Mama's titties alone for one morning," he told his child. EJ pouted and then laid on his chest in resignation as if he understood. Easy heard a giggle come from the bed.

"It's okay," Keona said, opening her eyes, "I'll get up."

"No, you're gonna sleep. If you aren't in any discomfort or pain, he can wait. When you're rested, I'll make you some food, and then you can nurse after if you want to. He'll be a'ight." Easy made his decree and left the room, heading downstairs.

EJ was fed in record time, and the two of them were on the couch playing with toys when Easy's cell phone dinged. He looked at the screen and used the app on his phone to disarm and unlock his front door. Moments later, Truck and King made it to the top of the stairs and into the living room.

Trevino "Truck" Davis and his cousin, Romelo "King" Davis were his business partners and best friends. They'd all known each other nearly all their lives, and when Romelo first started taking his corner boy beginnings to the next level, Easy and Truck were right behind him, protecting his interests and letting everyone know the King wouldn't be touched. Truck was his cousin's right hand and second-in-command, his chief enforcer and the deadliest threat in this corner of the world. Easy was right underneath Truck in the hierarchy, acting as an enforcer but also managing product distribution. He was proud to call them family, to learn from them and fight by their side.

Easy did want Keona to rest, but he'd also encouraged her extra sleep so he could talk to his friends without her protests. He knew she was trying to stay lowkey, but there was no way he wasn't calling King and Truck to the table. If whatever she was running from caught up to her, he needed to be ready. Trevino refastened the baby gate and faced him.

"Oh shit. You were serious?"

"Watch your language. And yes, I was serious, nigga. Why would I make this up?" Easy said to Truck, rolling his eyes.

Romelo laughed. "Damn, bro. You a whole dad out here. That's really your seed," he said.

"Can't deny him either," Truck said, sitting down next to EJ. "He look just like you, except for Keona's wild ass, unruly ass, Kelis from 'Milkshake' ass hair."

Romelo burst into more laughter.

"Leave my woman's hair alone," Easy said, an amused smirk on his face.

Truck grinned. "She's your woman again?"

"Come on. You know Key been mine since the day I met her. I wasn't the one who stopped believing it—she was. Now she's here, and as angry as I am at her, I'm also relieved she finally brought her ass home. And truth be told, when I'm holding my baby boy, it's hard to be angry at anything. He's here with me, where he belongs."

"And what about where Key belongs?" Truck continued. Easy shook his head.

"I ain't got time to play tug-of-war with her stubborn ass. She either gon trust me or she ain't. I've been all kinds of patient with her. I got her back now, and that's it. I wasn't expecting her to show up with EJ, though. Man, I wish she would have been honest with me two years ago. I missed my son's birth, his first steps, everything."

"You think the same thing that chased her out of here is why she's back?" Romelo asked. Easy nodded.

"I'm certain of it. I'm glad she's at least smart enough to know EJ is safer with me. I don't know how I'ma get her to realize it about herself, though. She's holding something back, something big. Plus, she's still trying to leave."

"Easy, you gotta make her stay. It ain't about what she want no more. You let her wild out for two years. She came back here, now she gotta deal with what's here," Romelo said, sitting on the couch too. EJ crawled into Trevino's lap, bouncing up and down and touching his face. Trevino tickled his stomach, and EJ exploded into laughter. Easy smiled. His son knew family when he saw it.

"Rome is right. She ain't have no business running out of here like she did, and I know you're pissed, but this is her home. With us. Key is yours like Nas is mine—ain't no getting away from it. It's why she's here. 'Cause truth be told, she could have disappeared with the youngin, with you none the wiser. She brought him here for a reason. She couldn't resist the pull of *home*," Trevino added, continuing his play with EJ.

"I know," Easy finally said, sighing, "but she still hasn't told me what she's so afraid of. I can't fix it until I know what's wrong."

"You can't force her to trust you, but maybe you can remind her what it's like when she does, and how it feels to *not* be scared all the time," Trevino said, playing peekaboo with EJ. Easy never thought he'd see the day when one of the most dangerous men he'd ever known was entertaining a baby. But recently, Trevino's first love Nasima had come home, joining him and his man Bashir in love, completing their home and relationship. Easy guessed the comfort and fulfillment was making him settle into family man mode faster.

"Trev is right," Romelo joined in again. "Tell her we can protect her. Y'all are family, and we're never letting anything happen to her or EJ."

"And make sure she hears you. We know you the quiet one who likes to let his actions speak, but women need to hear you say the words. Let her know who she got on her side. Remind her who you are," Trevino finished.

Easy sat back against the sofa, nodding. Maybe it was time to change his approach a little with Keona. He used to be content watching her be the bright, gregarious one in their relationship—the one who always had something to say. It was time for him to talk and her to listen.

"A'ight. I'll switch it up a little. Y'all make good points. I need her to let me in, and I know exactly how to start," Easy said. He decided to bombard Keona with his honesty, bare himself, and hopefully make her comfortable enough to do the same. And he was coming in hot, starting with the most powerful weapon in his arsenal: his beloved grandmother.

"I'm hungry. I thought this was a breakfast meeting," Romelo complained. Easy laughed and stood up.

"Sadie don't feed you?" he asked, referring to Romelo's woman. Romelo shrugged.

"I left too early, running out the door to see if you really had a baby over here."

"Nosy *and* hungry," Trevino laughed, pressing some keys on a toy keyboard. EJ clapped his hands. Easy went to the kitchen and started pulling out things to make breakfast for everyone. He heard a noise and turned, his breath catching.

Keona was standing on the stairs, looking like she didn't know if she should come down. She was barefoot, wearing leggings and one of his hoodies, her hair wild and free. Easy knew he was never getting the hoodie back, but she was so fine he didn't even care. Her body was covered, but the clothes didn't stop Easy from remembering it was wrapped in merely a towel the night before. He licked his lips, trying to focus. Key was a beautiful distraction, her face smooth and shining, hips and ass poking, her belly bouncing a little, her thighs magnificent. But the best part of her was still her delicious breasts, those soft pillows of sweetness, the hills with which she fed his son. Easy wanted them in his mouth, wanted to kiss her, make love to her, shake her for their two years of separation. Damn. Anger aside, he missed his woman.

"Come on down," he said softly, pushing down his thoughts. There would be time to hash things out later if he could convince Keona to stay. But for right now, he needed her to be comfortable and feel safe. "I'm about to make some food, and the fellas are here."

"Elliott—" Keona said in an alarmed whisper, but he cut her off.

"They're not gonna tell anyone you're here, Key. I wanted them to meet EJ, and you knew I would bring them in. You don't want to tell me what's going on, but I still need backup. Gotta protect my family. Now come eat," he said, his voice sharp. There wasn't going to be any more of this bullshit. Keeping things so close to the chest was hurting her, and Easy couldn't stand it anymore.

Keona stood there a moment longer, mouth open in shock at his directness and his tone. Then she came down the stairs without another word, going into the living room.

"Key! Come here, girl. Why you give this baby your wild ass hair?" Trevino said as he tossed EJ in the air and caught him again and again. EJ's hysterical laugh was contagious and Easy smiled. Keona shook her head and went to the couch, plopping down next to Romelo. The two of them hugged.

"Hi, Melo. It's good to see at least one of you," she said.

Romelo laughed. "What's going on, Key? I'm glad you're home."

"Never should have took your ass out of here, had my man all broken-hearted—"

"Truck," Easy stopped him. "Not now, okay?" Trevino shrugged and went back to amusing EJ. Keona closed her eyes and took a deep breath. Easy knew she was trying to get a hold of her emotions.

"It's okay, Elliott," she finally said. "I know it doesn't change anything, but I was broken-hearted too."

"It's cool. We got you back now. But back to my nephew's hair. What's going on? And he's what, sixteen months? The first cut is long overdue," Trevino said. Keona gasped and shook her head. She opened her arms to catch EJ, who had spotted her and opted to bounce back into her lap.

"Ain't no clippers going near my baby's head!"

"At the very least, we gotta shape it and line him up, Key," Easy said from the kitchen, where he was laying sausage patties in a pan. "You got my boy out here looking like we don't love him."

Keona grumbled. "He looks fine. He's just a baby."

"Woman, what did I say?" Easy said, putting his foot down again. Keona stared at him, surprise and desire coming into her eyes. Her warm pools of caramel pulled him in. Easy could stare into her eyes all day. *You like it when I boss up on you, huh,* he thought, smirking. He winked at her and went back to scrambling eggs.

Ten minutes later, they were all sitting at the table in the kitchen, wolfing down cheesy eggs, sage sausage, hash brown patties, and fruit. EJ sat on Romelo's lap and ate bits from his plate, then finally moved back to his mother. Keona had barely cleaned her plate before EJ was grabbing at her, looking for her breast. She excused herself to nurse him, and Easy stared longingly after them, wishing he was the one getting snuggled against her soft bosom. He shook his head to clear it. Imagine being jealous of his own son. He spent a few more minutes with his friends before seeing them out.

"Remember what we said: she belongs here with us. Make her stay, Easy," Romelo said. Easy nodded, dapping him up first, then Trevino. Time to get him and his woman back on the same page.

Easy locked up and went upstairs. Keona was in EJ's room, rubbing his back as he drifted off to sleep and settled into his very first nap in his new bed.

"I set up the monitor last night; you can see him from our room. Come talk to me for a minute," he told her, reaching to pull her up from the floor. If she had any thoughts about him calling it their room, she didn't voice them. They went into the master and settled next to each other in the bed, each lounging on their own side of the Vermont King they picked out together. Keona used to joke the bed was big enough for all their future children to sleep with them.

"I'm not gonna keep asking you what's going on with you, Keona. I want you to trust me enough to tell me, and I'm gonna show you that you can. But I am going to ask you to stay. I can protect you and you know it. Just like you know I'm gonna bury whoever wouldn't 'let' you come home and bring me my son."

"Elliott, you can't try to— If he hurt you, I— You need protection too. Who's going to protect you? I'd much rather you focus on keeping EJ safe. He's the priority. I don't deserve—"

"Don't even finish your sentence," Easy interrupted, scowling. "I don't know who this nigga is who got you so shook, but I'm not him. And my protection has never been and won't ever be conditional. You should know me—and yourself—better, Key. Am I still angry with you? Hell yeah. But there's no amount of anger that will keep me from doing what I've always done. You came back here for a reason other than EJ. You can fight it all you want, but we both know it. And you sit here with a straight face and ask me to keep our son safe and let you walk out there alone? You got me fucked up."

"Elliott, you shouldn't even want to talk to me after what I've done and what I put us through. I don't know why you're being so damn stubborn about this."

"Because it's what you need. You're not in charge anymore, and I will dismantle the shitty car you drove up in piece by piece to keep you here. Don't play with me, Key. Now, lay down with me and let's nap while EJ is napping. When we wake up, I'm taking y'all to MomMom's so she can meet her great-grandson." Easy finished and slid down onto the pillows. He pulled Keona closer until her head was on his chest and threw a blanket over them. He closed his eyes, inhaling the scent of his soap and her curl cream.

"Don't talk about my car," she said softly, and Easy chuckled, feeling better already.

Keona

Keona woke from her short nap horny and flushed. She'd been dreaming about her baby daddy. Dreaming of him kissing her, touching her, moving inside her. It was so real she'd come in her sleep. Now she was wet between her thighs, her breasts were heavy with desire and milk, and she was wrapped in his arms while he slept like he didn't have a care in the world. Keona needed to get up, but something about leaving Elliott's arms made her heart clench in protest. She'd been missing him terribly and her body knew it. Add in his dominant attitude and direct words from earlier and she was stuck, unwilling to move from his hold for any reason.

The previous night, they'd had their baby between them, so she hadn't felt the full joy and peace she was getting now, sleeping right up under him like she had so many nights before. He was even gently cupping her breast and caressing her nipple the way he used to, which definitely contributed to the orgasm she'd had in her sleep.

A whimper disturbed her thoughts, and she looked over at the baby monitor. EJ was awake and had moved off his low bed to the floor. He stood up, teetered, then fell on his butt again. He whined in annoyance, and the second louder noise was enough to wake his father. Elliott opened his almond eyes, looked at her, and smiled.

"You freshen up for MomMom's. I'll get him," he said and eased out of bed. Keona's first instinct was to object and demand he stay and baby her, but then she shook off her bratty attitude. Imagine being jealous of her own son. She got up and headed to the bathroom.

Thirty minutes later, they were all dressed, EJ was nursed, and they were on the way to MomMom's. Keona was nervous. The woman who raised Elliott didn't suffer fools and wouldn't take it easy on her. She had to own up to what she'd done and everything she hadn't told Elliott about it. When they pulled up, she hesitated, her hand shaking a little on the door handle.

"She's not angry with you, Key," Elliott whispered, leaning over to comfort her. "She was more pissed at me for not going after you, truth be told. You're fine, and you're still family." His words settled Keona, and she got out of the car, ready to face the music.

Nanette "MomMom" Tanner was a commanding woman, about Keona's height and build, with rich dark skin, a wide smile, and long gray hair. She also shared Elliott's big almond-colored eyes. She pulled Keona in for a long hug, rocking her back and forth. Keona immediately burst into tears, the comfort too much for her frazzled nerves.

"It's alright, my baby." MomMom rubbed her back. "It's alright. You're home now. I knew you'd come home."

Keona sobbed, knowing Elliott was watching, knowing he could see her pain and fear on full display. But she didn't care, she couldn't care. She'd been missing this feeling for two years and every day had seemed longer than the one before it. EJ whimpered and Keona realized her tears were probably scaring him. *And his father,* she thought, remembering how helpless Elliott always felt when she cried. She pulled back, wiping her face and sniffling.

"I'm sorry. I'm so...happy to see you," she said softly. MomMom laughed.

"Likewise, my baby. I've been waiting a long time for you. And you brought me a surprise, I see."

"Yeah." Elliott stepped up, their son in his arms. "This is EJ, your great-grandson."

MomMom held out her arms, and after a moment of silent contemplation, EJ threw himself into them. She cradled him against her, whispering in his ear, and Keona smiled. Elliott reached for her hand, and she gave it to him, a calm settling over her. Maybe it wasn't so bad letting people know she was home.

"Keona, leave him be," MomMom said as EJ toddled around her living room. His steps were hesitant, wobbly and unsure, and he fell on his bottom often. Keona knew it was because she was always carrying him instead of letting him get stronger and steadier at walking. Elliott had moved the coffee table against a wall and laid out a blanket and a bunch of toys Keona hadn't even realized he brought with them. Now he was in the kitchen checking in with Truck and would be ordering lunch after. Keona watched her baby, fighting the urge to pick him up and cradle him.

"I don't want him to hurt himself or break something," she said. MomMom laughed.

"He's fine, baby. You've got to relax. He's got both our eyes on him."

"I know, you're right. I'm "

"It's been lonely for you, hasn't it?" MomMom said, taking Keona's hands in hers. Elliott's grandmother had been more of a parent than either of hers, and she'd been missed. Her soft hands were like a balm for Keona's sensitive nerves.

"How did you know?" she whispered now. MomMom smiled gently.

"You barely let him walk, always cradling him. You won't wean him. You're holding him so tight, baby. Holding him like he's the only thing you have. It's been lonely, hasn't it?"

"Yes, ma'am," Keona admitted, tears sliding down her face. Would she ever stop crying? MomMom patted her hand again and kissed her cheek.

"You're okay, you're back with your family now," she said. Keona nodded.

"I am...but I can't stay. I mean I shouldn't stay; it's complicated."

"Complicated or not, I know you don't think my grandson is letting you leave him again."

"He doesn't want to, but he doesn't know everything. If he did—"

"Seems to me if he doesn't know all he needs to know, you can fix it by telling him," MomMom pointed out.

Keona sighed. She knew she owed Elliott an explanation—a real one—but the more she thought of her father's cruelty, the more she felt like no one else needed to be exposed to the kind of man he could be. Her beloved Elliott would be off his radar if she stayed away. But the more her man touched her, held her, looked at her with his almond gaze and told her how things were going to be, the more she wanted to lay up under him forever and have all his babies. Could she risk telling Elliott everything? Would he still want her if he knew?

"I don't know what to do, MomMom," Keona said, feeling out of sorts and uneasy. MomMom nodded.

"You give Elliott what he's been giving you, baby. Trust him. If you care for him, trust him."

"I love him more than anything except our son," Keona said, trying to keep more tears from falling. "I've hurt him so much, and I didn't mean to. I'm not trying to."

"Keona, baby, you're contemplating walking out on him *again* for the same reason you did the first time, and you're still silent about the real explanation. If you're not trying to hurt him, what *are* you trying to do?" MomMom asked. Keona sniffed, wiping her face with her free hand.

"I'm trying to protect him. If anything happened to you, or to him, because of me, I would die. I would be broken."

"And if something happened to you because you were out there trying to fight a battle alone instead of with your family, what do you think would happen to Elliott? Do you really think he'd survive losing you? Especially if he lost you because you were off on your own when you could have trusted him?"

After MomMom finished, Keona sat there, warring with herself. She could almost feel the relief of unburdening herself to Elliott, the sheer calm from allowing him to protect her and solve the problem. But then the fear bubbled up, like heartburn after a good meal, and she was cold all over. What if her father did what he promised two years ago? Elliott was strong, capable, and brave, but he wasn't a superhero. He didn't have long enough arms to wrap around all of them, and it felt like too much to ask of him. But MomMom seemed so sure. Was trusting him the answer?

"Did he ask you to talk to me?" she finally said aloud, pointing to the kitchen where Elliott was on the phone. MomMom smiled.

"No. But that don't mean I don't know when he needs me to," she responded with a wink. Keona laughed a little. EJ stacked blocks on top of one another, knocking them down when they got to a certain height and cracking himself up. She stared at him, her heart lighter. He made everything better. He was her priority. EJ was the reason, and she'd do anything for him.

"I can't let anything happen to him," she said, still looking at her son.

"Then lean on his family, baby. You have support, use it," MomMom insisted.

Keona sighed. Maybe she could. Because as much as she didn't want to admit it, her baby daddy was right. EJ wasn't the only reason she'd run to Elliott. She was here because he was home, plain and simple. Because he was the one place she could rest, the one place she could be. Maybe it was time to tell him everything.

Elliott walked back into the room, putting his cell phone in his pocket. He came over to them and kissed her softly on the lips, surprising her. The desire she'd felt lying in his arms came back swiftly and surely, heating her entire body. *How did he do that?* He pulled off his sneakers and got down on the floor with their son, helping him stack blocks and knock them over. Keona wanted to cry again. She'd never seen anything so beautiful.

"You don't want to miss a moment of this, trust me," Mom-Mom's voice drifted into her ear. "You don't get this time with them back, Keona. Trust your heart and your instincts. Bet on my grandson; I promise you won't lose."

Back at the house, Elliott laid EJ in his bed for a short nap, then pulled her into their bedroom where they could talk privately but still hear their son. Elliott took off his shoes and got into bed, sitting on the mountain of pillows at the headboard. He opened his arms and Keona took off her shoes before climbing into them. He settled her between his open legs, her back against his chest, his nose in her hair.

"I'm so angry with you, Key," Elliott whispered, running his fingers up and down her arms. "I am so fucking mad you walked out on me. Even madder you were pregnant when you did it, and I missed two years of my son's life—"

"Elliott—" Keona interrupted, trying to push out of his arms. He stopped her, holding her still. He continued talking, soothing her with his voice.

"But even when I'm angry, I can't help wanting you in my arms. I can't help feeling like you're supposed to be here with me, like this is your rightful place."

"I didn't want to go. You have to believe me, baby. I didn't want to. I'm sorry."

"You use the same hair cream," he whispered, changing the subject abruptly. Keona closed her eyes, held his hand. He remembered.

"Some things don't change, Elliott."

"You're right. You know what else hasn't changed? You and me. You were mine, and you're still mine. Why do you think those other bedrooms are still empty? This is your house, Key, your life. I've been waiting for you to come back to it."

"Why? The way I left was—why would you wait for me?" she asked incredulously. Elliott laughed softly.

"I know I don't say much, so you were always surprised at the ways I knew you, the ways I could read you. The day you left...I could see in your eyes you were afraid of something. I was angry at you leaving, but even more angry because you didn't feel like you could tell me what was chasing you out of here. I waited for you because I hoped you'd fight whatever it was and come back. I know now I should have gone after you...and for that, I'm sorry. I'm sorry for being too angry to react to how scared you must have been."

At the end of his words, Keona felt tears sliding down her cheeks. Elliott wasn't a huge talker, more content to let her speak for them as a couple and let his actions show how he felt. Keona never minded because he was so good, she never once doubted his love, but hearing him speak about them blew her away. Her Elliott, expressing himself like this? The silent watcher speaking so knowledgeably about her heart and her emotions was so much, almost too much. God, she loved this man. He'd never given up on her or on them.

"Oh, Elliott, I missed you so much. If it were up to me, I'd have chained myself to you. I never wanted anything but our life, our love, our babies," she whispered through her tears. He held her tighter.

"Neither did I. It's why I haven't moved on or even tried to...and why I haven't been with anyone else."

She turned to face him. "What? What do you mean?"

"I mean what I said. I haven't touched anyone in two years. I only wanted my woman—I only wanted you."

"But Laney—"

"Laney hasn't been anywhere near my dick, Keona," Elliott cut her off with a frown. "I'm a lot of things, but I respect the code. If I *was* gonna move on, why would it be with your friend?"

"I'm not saying— Laney told me— She said you were 'very well taken care of' and I didn't need to worry about you anymore," Keona explained. Elliott shook his head.

"She said that shit to make you mad, baby. I don't deal with anyone at all, and especially not Laney. We suspected one of our runners was skimming off the top and he was avoiding us; he's a regular at Laney's bar, so she said she'd look out for him. She came over here to give me *information*, baby, nothing else. And the only reason she answered the door was because I was expecting Truck; I assumed you were him and told Laney to let him in on her way out."

Keona relaxed, believing him. It was very much like Laney to mess with her head, and she knew if Elliott was with Laney, he'd be loyal to her and would have stood up for her.

"I hurt Laney too when I left the way I did. I shouldn't be surprised she'd try to hurt me back."

"Yeah, but it still wasn't cool to say those things. She don't know shit about how I'm being taken care of."

Keona sat back against him again, sighing. The feeling of Elliott's hands on her, his warm breath moving her hair, his firm body holding hers, was all she needed in the world. He'd laid open so much to her today, first with his grandmother and now in this conversation. This man loved her like no other, and her heart wouldn't recognize anyone else. What kind of life was she destined to live running away from him again? All the things she believed about him and EJ's safety were still true and always at the edge of her mind. But how long could she run? The rest of her life? Maybe it was time to stand and fight. Maybe it was time to ask Elliott to fight with her.

"Baby..." Keona whispered to him. Elliott stopped humming to himself and focused on her.

"Yes, love?"

"Two years ago...my father found out where I was and came looking for me. He'd been leaving me alone for years; I almost forgot he was still out there somewhere. But he came for me, said it was time to get a return on his investment. I didn't want to go, I swear. But he told me— He said he'd—"

"Key, calm down. Breathe, baby. Start from the beginning. Why did he come for you?"

"His organization traffics everything they can—stolen goods, drugs, weapons, even women and children. Two years ago, something went wrong with his operation, and he needed capital to rebuild. His potential new partner wanted me to be part of the deal. My father came for me, said I had to do it. I told him no, but then he showed me...he had surveillance, Elliott. You, MomMom, her friends. He said he'd hurt you if I didn't go. He'd kill you both slowly and make me watch."

"Oh, my baby," Elliott whispered, his voice strained. "I'm so sorry."

Keona was crying again, but she couldn't stop now. She couldn't stop until her man knew she'd never break his heart on purpose. Keona sat up, turning in his arms and straddling his lap. Elliott made room for her thickness, holding her tightly.

"I went with him; I didn't know what else to do. But things got worse for me when we got back to his compound. The deal he wanted so badly fell through—"

"Because they found out you were pregnant," Elliott finished for her. Keona nodded.

"Our son saved my life. Then my father started thinking of EJ as his real legacy. He kept me prisoner after, told me I had to stay until EJ was walking and talking. Then he'd keep him and get rid of me somehow. Mae, his housekeeper, felt sorry for me; she was the only one who treated me with any kindness. I was locked in my own quarters almost the entire pregnancy. She was the only one I was allowed to see and talk to. He wouldn't even take me to the hospital; he brought in a doctor every couple of months until I delivered. I had EJ at his house, with Mae holding my hand."

"When EJ was six months old, my father started letting me come out again, parading me in front of potential 'investors,' hoping to find someone I would be of value to. He would hit me whenever I wasn't charming enough, call me worthless and say I was like my mother. It made me sick, but I had to protect our son. He said he would take him away if I didn't do it."

"What happened two days ago, Keona? Why'd you come here?" Elliott asked, his voice tight and filled with rage. Keona almost wanted to stop there, but she knew she couldn't. She sniffed, wiped her face.

"The truth is, I'd been trying to put together an escape plan for a while. When my father left to make some pickup, I knew it might be my only chance. The night before he left, I heard him and a friend of his talking. He said maybe it was time to put me to work like the other girls, make me service clients and take EJ away because I was too attached to him. Forcing his own daughter into prostitution was bad enough, but I couldn't let him take EJ. It was all the motivation I needed. Mae is the one who usually watches me while he's gone. When I told her what they were planning, she said it was too far and she wasn't going to be a part of it. As soon as he was gone, I packed. She promised to help me leave, and she did."

"How did she do it?" Elliott asked.

"Mae turned off the power and turned it on again, forcing a system reboot. It shut down the alarms in the house and at the gate, giving me twenty minutes to leave."

"What about cameras?" Elliott continued. Keona shook her head.

"There aren't many inside the house. The outside and the property perimeter have most of the cameras, and they were rebooting too."

"Doesn't he have people watching the house?"

"There are only two guards, and they were preoccupied with making sure no one used the reboot to get *on* the property. There's a smaller gate on the east side of the house and I drove out of it," Keona explained further.

"When will he realize you're gone?"

"He'll be home in five days, but it could be sooner. I figured I would come here, get you to take EJ—"

"And get a five-day head start. Where were you going to go, Key?"

"I don't know, Elliott. I just needed to get far away. The Wolf doesn't—"

"Wait a minute. What did you say?" Elliott stopped her with a question. Keona shrugged.

"My father. They call him *The Wolf*," she replied. Elliott cursed and pulled her to him, rocking her in his arms. When he pulled back, his big eyes were filled with sadness and remorse.

"Shit. I'm so sorry, my love. This is on me. I'm so sorry," he said. Keona pressed her lips to his, trying to calm him, to get the sad look off his face.

"No, baby. It's okay. I'm alright. It's been hard, but—"

"That's not what I mean, Key. I mean the reason this whole thing happened is because of me. If I'd paid attention—fuck. I knew you had the same last name, but it's a common one. Our intel didn't say he had a daughter, but if he abandoned you, it makes sense—"

"Elliott, *you're* not making sense. Why is this your fault?" Keona interrupted. He sighed, shaking his head.

"The Wolf is your father. Kenyon Ross, The Wolf, is your father," he started.

"Yes, his name is—wait. You know him?"

Elliott nodded. "Yes, baby, I know him. And him finding you may have been all my fault."

3

Chapter Three

Easy sighed, trying to calm himself. He knew Keona's whole story would be one he didn't want to hear, but he'd never imagined learning he was the cause of her pain. She sat in his lap, staring at him, her caramel eyes fearful and sad. She was dreading what he had to say. Easy was dreading it too. But they needed to get the entire story out or they'd never be able to move forward. He was also hesitant because he never shared this much of his work with Keona. He normally kept her out of the inner workings of his "job" and Romelo's operation. It was safer. But he knew he'd have to tell Melo Keona was The Wolf's daughter. If he was going to put her out there, he had to put himself out there too.

"Two years ago, The Wolf tried to come for Romelo's territory in the west. He and his crew had been coming at us for a while; they thought we were the weakest there. Now previously, they robbed a couple of workers, stole a shipment, tried to cause some small trouble, poke at us first. Two years ago, they came in heavy right away; they wanted an all-out war with us. The Wolf came at us hard and fast, thinking he had surprise on his side."

"What happened?" Keona asked, reaching up to caress the side of his face. Easy closed his eyes, loving her touch.

"Truck is the best at what he does, that's what happened. He anticipated something new and heavy—they'd been too quiet, and he was suspicious—so we were ready. We mangled them, babe. Caught them completely off guard with the counterattack. We put ten of your father's top soldiers in the dirt, and Truck took out three of his four lieutenants before he retreated. His need to re-build was because of us. He went underground and we had other priorities, so we didn't go after him. But we've been watching on and off, trying to see when he'd come for us again. Truck has been adamant we need to take him out too."

Keona threw her arms around his neck, snuggling closer. Easy rubbed her soft body, breathing in the scent of her hair.

"I'm so glad you're okay, baby. If he'd hurt you—" she whispered.

"He didn't even get close enough, love. Don't worry about me. I'm fine, and we're all good," Easy assured her. He planted soft kisses on her neck, and she sighed softly, melting into his touch. Then Keona pulled back, her eyes curious.

"Elliott, I still don't understand why you would say this was your fault."

"Research, baby. You want to know your enemy, you do your research. You said your father had been leaving you alone for years. It's probably because he never bothered to look for you. He most likely found you when he was looking into Romelo's opera-tion—and me, babe. You and MomMom got on his radar because of me. I'm so sorry, Keona. I'm sorry, baby."

"No, no, it's not your fault, Elliott. It's still mine," Keona in-sisted, shaking her head. "If I'd told you who he was a long time ago, none of this would have happened. I fucked up *your* intel by not being honest with you and not trusting you. Baby, I risked your life—"

"Key, I'm right here. And you're right here. I don't want to throw blame anymore. And I need you to promise you're going to trust me from now on. Promise me you're in this with me, and you'll let me protect you and EJ. Let me do what I know how to do."

"I'll never leave you again, baby. I promise," Keona said urgently. She pressed her lips to his and Easy moaned, tangling one hand in her curly hair. Her lips were still as soft as he remembered, fitting with his perfectly. His other hand rubbed her lower back and full bottom, squeezing the generous bounty. Their mouths fused sensually, moving over each other with intent and passion. Keona ran her hands over his shoulders and back as they tasted each other. Easy sucked on her lower lip, using her gasp of pleasure to slide his tongue into her mouth. His tongue found hers, tangled with it, taking the kiss deeper. His dick hardened, lengthened, and he pushed against her softness, desperate to bury himself inside her.

"Mama! Dada!" An indignant yell, then a whine interrupted them, and Easy and Keona separated their mouths, both glancing at the baby monitor. EJ was out of bed, throwing toys around his room, clearly unhappy about waking up alone. Keona giggled. Easy groaned. Being interrupted was something he and Keona weren't dealing with before. Parenthood was a whole new world indeed.

"I'll get him," she said, climbing off his lap. He nodded, giving her one last kiss. Easy looked at her, all her plentiful jiggle barely contained in her leggings and graphic t-shirt. Her hips and thighs spread even farther now because of their son; her waist wasn't as wide but still thick, and her belly bulged a bit. Her titties were juicy mounds no bra could contain and the folds in her back and arms felt like home to him. His thick ass baby mama was even thicker now, so deliciously plush, and he couldn't wait to make love to her.

"Want me to start some dinner?" he asked. Keona smiled and shook her head.

"No, not yet. I can give him a snack and he can play in the living room while we talk some more."

"I want to do more than talk, Mama."

"The 'more' will have to wait until he's down for the night, Daddy," she said back, blowing him a kiss and leaving their room. Easy adjusted himself in his pants, trying to get his dick to calm down. He was okay again by the time she came back with EJ, holding his hand as he walked in on his chubby legs.

"Dada!" he yelled. Easy smiled and got up, scooping EJ into his arms. He kissed his son's face, making him giggle.

"You have a good nap, baby boy?" he asked. EJ nodded, rubbing his father's face in his hands, and Easy laughed. The three of them headed downstairs, where Keona gave EJ a yogurt pouch, two mini muffins, and a banana, the last of the things she'd bought for the road trip here. Then they all went to the living room.

"Key, do you mind making a grocery list for him? Once I get the hang of the way he eats, I can take care of it—"

"You don't have to do that, Elliott," Keona interrupted, untangling two toys from each other and giving them back to EJ.

"Do what, help you? Of course, I do."

"No, I mean you don't have to take on everything with EJ now, like you're making it up to me because I've been taking care of him by myself. We'll share the load; he's *our* son."

"But I want you to get more rest. When you and MomMom were talking, I was reading up on how exhausting it is to be a nursing mom. You need to be eating when he eats and sleeping when he sleeps. I'm gonna make sure you keep your energy up," Easy said. Keona grinned at him and reached out her hand, pulling him down on the floor next to her. She leaned against his chest, releasing a deep breath.

"I've missed the way you love me. So focused and warm. You didn't say much, Elliott, but I felt it. I felt every bit of your love, and I missed it," she said to him, her voice low and shaky like she wanted to cry again. Easy kissed her forehead.

"You're home now, baby. You'll never miss me again. I'm going to take care of everything," he promised. He felt confident reassuring Keona because he finally felt like he had all the information he needed. The Wolf wouldn't walk away from their next encounter, especially now that Easy knew how his family had been treated at his hands. A man who would sell his daughter and grandson wasn't a man worthy of mercy, and Easy didn't plan on giving him any.

"I don't want you to get hurt, Elliott. He can't hurt you," Keona insisted. Easy kissed the side of her face, calming her.

"He won't. But I need your help, mama. I need you to tell Romelo and Trevino everything you know about the compound where you were and your father's business. Can you do that for me?"

"Of course, baby. I'll tell them everything," Keona promised.

"Dada, pway!" EJ called out, bringing Easy a toy. He laughed at his son and took the toy, shifting so he could play with him. His cell phone rang, and he grabbed it with one hand while he rammed toy cars into block stacks with the other. EJ's laughter rang in the background as he answered Romelo.

"Yo," Easy greeted.

"Yeah, I got your text. You need a meeting?"

"Yeah. Key told me what I needed to know, and now you need to hear it too—you and Truck."

"I'll be right there. Key cool with me bringing Sadie?" Romelo asked. Easy nudged Keona and she lifted her eyes to his.

"Melo is on his way, but he wants to bring Sadie. You good with company?" he asked her. Keona's brows furrowed in confusion and Easy mimed he would explain later.

"Sure," she said, "I'd love to see Sadie." Easy smiled back.

"Bring the wifey, it's cool. I'll order some food for us," he said into the phone.

"Perfect. Be there in thirty," Romelo said and hung up. Easy put his phone down, focusing his attention on the game he was playing with his son. Truck would call him next.

"Wifey? Sadie? Where's Bianca?" Keona wondered. Easy shook his head. His baby had missed a lot.

"She left about a year ago; she said she needed space to follow her dreams. Melo and Sadie were pretty broken up about it, and they kinda sought comfort...in each other. Now, they're stuck like glue. I know it seems strange, but it's real between them."

"Wow. I'm glad they're both okay, though," Keona commented. She sighed, and Easy knew she was still sorting out her feelings over leaving him and hurting his heart. He knew Bianca acted rashly, like Keona had, and he hoped, like his woman, she'd eventually have the sense to bring her ass home.

"I'm sure Sadie will tell me all about it. What kind of food should we get?" Keona asked, sitting up straight and shaking off her emotions. Easy kissed her cheek.

"Don't let Bianca's shit get in your head. You're home now, Key. Let's focus on keeping you here and keeping you and EJ safe. Nothing else matters anymore. I'll order lasagna or baked ziti, something easy. We can get salad and bread, some dessert, and make it a family night. Truck can bring Bash and Nasima. If Sadie's coming, I figure you'll want to see them too."

"Wait. Bianca left and Nasima came home?" Keona turned to him, her eyes wide. Easy nodded.

"Yup. And found her way right back to Truck where she belongs. She, Truck, and Bash are all together now. She completes them, and lowkey, Bash might be more in love than Trevino." He laughed as he finished, remembering seeing Nas at the gym and Bash's mood whenever she smiled at or talked to anyone else. Keona looked curious.

"Aww. Their deciding to be together is wonderful. Although, from what I remember from way back in the day, I don't think it's possible for someone to love Nas more than Trevino."

Easy laughed again. "Wait until you see them together."

"I'm glad she's back. We spoke a few times in the years she was away. She seemed fine...until Tone. But I could tell home was clearly where her heart was," she said, frowning when she referred to Nasima's ex-boyfriend.

Easy gathered his son to him with one arm and pulled his baby mama close with the other. They fit perfectly with him. His family.

"And yours? Was home where you left your heart too?" he whispered to Keona. She reached up, stroked his face, stared into his eyes.

"Why do you think I came back to get it?" she whispered back. Easy kissed her, moaning into her mouth, taking her sweet lips. Keona whimpered, trying to move closer. Their mouths clung, tasting, and Easy rubbed her soft titties. He couldn't wait until it was time to put their son down for the night. His cell phone rang again, and he pulled back, turning to grab the phone from EJ, who had crawled out of his arms while he kissed Keona.

"Yo."

"Yeah?" Truck said.

"Dinner in thirty minutes. Bring Nas and Bash. I have news, and you need it."

"Oh, word? We're on our way," Truck said and hung up. Keona was changing EJ and looked up at him, trying to mask the worry on her face. Easy saw it anyway.

"I told you I'm taking care of it, didn't I?" he said softly. She nodded, standing EJ up without his pants and letting him go back to the toys in his diaper and shirt.

"Yes, baby, you did."

"Then trust me, woman," he said, leaning over to kiss her mouth again and again. "You hear me? You promised."

"I did," Keona said between his kisses. "I did promise, and I do trust you."

Easy smirked, turning for a second to take the toy EJ was handing him. He kissed Keona once more, making her moan and cling to him.

"You sexy as hell when you believe in me, mama," he said, chuckling softly. "And I'm making up for all my lost time tonight, so get ready."

Keona

"Key, why don't you tell us to go home so you can fuck your man already?" Sadie said with a laugh.

She, Sadie, and Nasima sat at the kitchen table, catching up with each other. Nasima had shared the entire story of Trevino and Bashir's plan to make her a part of their lives, and Sadie caught her up on Bianca leaving and her and Romelo drifting to each other afterward. She jumped a little, turning to face the two women.

"Huh? What?"

"You are drooling over there, staring at Easy like he's the lasagna we ate earlier. Cut the night short, boo. You're the woman of this house," Nasima said, giggling too.

Keona ducked her head, embarrassed. Her baby daddy was as fine as he could be, and she was ready to be spread out underneath him. He sat in the living room with the rest of the guys, talking about strategy and logistical options. Bash was holding EJ in his arms as he tuned into the conversation. He wasn't in the organization, but everyone trusted him implicitly. Her son was hilarious, jerking himself awake every time he drifted off, determined not to miss a thing. He'd had a full day, and Keona was ready to get him and nurse him into the deepest sleep so she could reunite with his daddy the right way.

After a lively dinner and reunion, Elliott sat next to her on the couch and held her hand while she told Romelo and Trevino where her father's house was and as much as she could remember about his business and security layout. She wasn't privy to much, but she told them everything she did know without hesitation. Her father only wanted to use her and had only sought her out to punish Elliott. She'd been a prisoner, forced into loneliness, her son's safety hinging on her obedience and willingness to sell herself. Keona had no qualms about choosing her man over him because he could have simply left her alone, the way he'd done her entire life. Elliott and EJ were the priority now.

Staring at Elliott, watching his long fingers move over maps and papers on the coffee table as he spoke confidently about eliminating this threat for all of them, Keona was wet and tingly all over. She wanted her man. She needed him.

"He's so fine it's ridiculous," she said, tuning back into the ladies. "I barely kept my hands off him before we were apart. Two years of missing him only amplified things."

"Don't get me started. You know how long I was away from Vino. I want to be in his skin these days. And Bash makes me… Shit, maybe it is time for us to go home," Nasima said, fanning her face. Keona laughed.

"Romelo left early this morning and was out all day. I didn't see him until he picked me up to come over here. I got plans for his ass," Sadie declared, licking her lips. Keona looked at the ladies, then made her decision. She stood up, marching into the living room. She scooped EJ up from Bash's arms and held him on her hip.

"It's past EJ's bedtime, and y'all have had my man long enough," she said to the group. The four men looked up, surprised. Bashir laughed under his breath and Elliott smirked, amused.

"You putting us out, Key?" Trevino said, grinning. Keona nodded.

"I sure am. Y'all know how I love you, but us women are feeling neglected, and baby boy needs story time with his dad."

"Okay, Mama. You're right. Let's pick this up tomorrow. I'll come to the office," Elliott agreed, standing up.

Nasima came into the living room and gestured to her two men with a smile. They got up like they were tethered to her, gathering their things and saying goodbye. Sadie drifted in, standing behind Romelo and leaning down to whisper in his ear. He stood up, his smile huge.

"Meeting in the office tomorrow—not early, though," he said, grabbing his lover's hand. A few minutes later, the living room was empty and the house was locked up tight. Elliott came to her, taking EJ from her arms and kissing her.

"You something else, you know that?" he said.

Keona winked and turned off the lights, moving the baby gate so Elliott could follow her upstairs. EJ was drifting, so they settled for a good wipe down instead of a full bath. He nursed and was asleep as soon as they laid him in his bed. Elliott grabbed her hand and pulled her into their room, then the en suite bathroom.

"You want a bath?" he asked. Keona shook her head. She knew Elliott was trying to romance her, ease her into lovemaking since it'd been so long, but she wanted her man's hands and mouth on her. She needed Elliott Tanner to give her what she'd been missing.

"A shower will do...if you get in with me," she said, pulling her top over her head. Elliott copied her and got rid of his pants too. His dick was hard but not fully, and she was still hypnotized by his length and girth. She'd missed her friend. Keona undid the clasp of her bra and her breasts jiggled free, plopping onto her stomach. She thought about covering up—she'd thickened even more since having the baby—but the look in Elliott's eyes stopped her. He was staring at her with nothing but complete lust and fascination. He pulled her close and swooped down, covering her mouth with his. Keona gasped and then moaned, relaxing into him.

Their kiss was filled with longing, scorching with their need, and coated with two years of missing and wanting each other. Keona had never felt so desired and so safe. Elliott could make anything better for her. He grabbed the sides of her belly, pulling her into him, letting her feel his hardness, his need for her. Keona raised up on her toes, throwing her arms around his neck, desperate to be closer. The wet smacks of their deep kisses and the moans accompanying them were all that could be heard in the bathroom. Elliott leaned down and moved his hands to cuff her bottom, keeping up the sensual plunder of her lips and tongue.

Keona stepped back, licking her lips. She tugged Elliott's hand, pulling him to the huge shower with her, then turned away to start and adjust the water. Elliott pulled her leggings and underwear down from behind her, helping her step out of them. He massaged her full bottom and kissed the round globes of her ass, making her shiver. Elliott let his mouth guide him down her big thighs, the back of her kneecaps, her thick calves. The water steamed up the bathroom as Keona stood there, sighing with pleasure as her man reacquainted himself with her body.

"I've missed you, Lollipop," he whispered, slipping back into the love name he'd given her. Keona almost cried. He really did miss her. She never thought she'd hear him call her his Lollipop again.

"Baby, I've missed you too," she whispered back. He stood up straight and pulled her into the shower, closing the door behind them. They fell into each other, kissing urgently as water sprayed their bodies. The shower was designed with wall jets and an over-arching showerhead. Steamy water fell around them like they were naked in a storm. Keona felt a rush inside her, love and lust swirling within, and knew the storm was just beginning.

Elliott pulled back, grabbing an exfoliating sponge from the ledge beside him. He squirted lemon and verbena body wash into it, then moved it over her skin slowly, never taking his eyes from hers. His almond-colored orbs filled with love and desire and Keona had never seen anything so beautiful. Having those eyes gifted to her son only made them more special in her mind. Her man washed her thoroughly, making her moan when he swirled the sponge around her nipples and over her pussy. Keona took the sponge, rinsed it, and re-lathered, returning the favor. Elliott's amazing dick was fully hard now, poking her stomach, seeking entrance into her wetness. They kissed again as the water rinsed them both, then shut the shower off, grabbing towels and heading into the bedroom area.

"I don't know how I survived without you in my arms, Lollipop," Elliott said, drying her. "This body has been in my dreams every night, leaving me cold and sick when I woke up and you weren't there. I know now I can't live without you, Key. Please don't make me."

"Elliott, you are my home, and I am so sorry I left you doubting. I was afraid, and I had reason to be, but I had no reason to believe you wouldn't move heaven and earth to protect me because you always have. But I hope you can believe my heart never left you, baby. And I was sick too, even more so whenever I held our son and spoke about you. I was finding my way home, Elliott. I promise you I was. We'll never live without each other again, no matter what happens."

"I'm never gonna play about mine. I will eliminate any threat to you and EJ, no matter what I have to do."

His words made her pulse race, her heart pound. His protectiveness and strength set her entire body on fire, and she was tired of waiting.

"Make love to me, Elliott. I need you," Keona said to her man. She rubbed a towel over his shoulders and chest, moving in to kiss his nipples when she was done. Elliott groaned and tangled his hand in her thick, damp coils as she moved her mouth back and forth. Keona gripped his dick in her hands, massaging him, introducing herself all over again. It had been so long. Elliott growled and pushed her back onto the bed, crawling on top and spreading her thighs. He entered her in one smooth thrust, groaning at her dripping tightness. Keona cried out, the invasion almost too much, but her body adjusted quickly to what it knew, to what was hers.

"I'm sorry, Lollipop," Elliott said, holding still to give her a minute. "I won't be so rough again. I needed you so much. I'm sorry."

Keona shook her head, covered his mouth with her hands. "I'm okay, baby. I needed you too."

Elliott nodded and began to move, his dick filling her over and over, her pussy clenching around him every time he sank inside again. Keona whimpered, lifted her hips, and followed his rhythm. The flat of his tongue slid over her fingers, which were still covering his mouth. Elliott sucked them as he fucked her hard, his eyes closed.

"Elliott, I love you," Keona gasped out, tears leaking from her eyes. His dick was magic, wiping away two years of loneliness and cold. All she ever needed was this man inside her and his babies to raise. They were a perfect fit, their flow undeniable, their bodies completely in sync. Keona wanted more. She wanted forever.

"I love you too, Lollipop. I love you so much," Elliott said back.

"More, Elliott, please give me more," she whined. Elliott nodded, continuing his ravaging, fucking her senseless. His hand moved between them and stroked her clit, playing in her wetness. Keona screamed, her orgasm slamming into her, leaving her dazed and breathless. She jerked as her pussy pulsed over and over, her cream leaking. The pleasure washing over her was staggering, and she wanted a replay.

"Gotdamn, Key. You wet us both up, baby. You missed me, huh? You missed Daddy?" Elliott said, his lustful gaze full of arrogance. Keona smiled.

"Yes, baby." She told the truth without an ounce of shame. "I missed you bad."

"Then you gon take this dick until I can't give you no more, hear me?" he said, thrusting again, daring her to deny him. Keona whimpered and nodded her head.

"Yes, I'm gonna take it," she moaned. Elliott leaned down to kiss her, sucking at her lips and sliding his tongue between them. He started fucking her again, hitting her spot deep inside and making her shake. His mouth drifted from her neck down to her breasts and he adjusted his position to catch her nipple with his tongue. He suckled her, moaning low.

Keona panted and dug her nails into him. "Not too hard, or I'll squirt milk."

Elliott laughed. "Then I guess baby boy will need to learn how to share." He did it again, loving her sweet moans of pleasure. They moved together, moaning and groaning, whispering words of love and need. There was magic in the way they touched, and Keona could feel it filling her life again, making her limbs tingle and her heart pound. With every touch of Elliott's hands and mouth, she was reborn in love. And after two long years, she couldn't get enough.

"Have my baby, Lollipop," Elliott said, pulling out to the tip before sliding in again. Keona's soft cries were filled with desperation. All she wanted was more, and she could barely focus on her man's words. *A baby?* Her thoughts were tangled, but she could have sworn they had one sleeping in the next room.

"Baby, I already did," she replied, hoping it was the right answer. Her brain was trying to catch up. Elliott chuckled.

"Then have another one. Give me another one, please," he begged while he fucked her. It was pure fire, pure pleasure...pure madness because Keona didn't think twice before she responded.

"Yes, Elliott, I'll have your baby. I'll have all your babies."

"You sure, Lollipop? Cause you about to get them all."

"Yes, I'm sure. Give me all your babies," she demanded. Elliott held her thighs up, pounding into her. Keona climaxed, calling his name, crying for mercy. Elliott groaned and gripped her legs so hard she knew she'd still feel it in the morning.

"Fuck!" he yelled out as his nut coated her pussy, warm and thick. He came so hard, so much, murmuring her name under his breath like a prayer. Elliott fell on top of her and gathered her into his arms. She was asleep moments later.

4

Chapter Four

Easy

Easy pulled out of Keona, moving to the side of her. She'd passed out, her hair wild and her edges sweated, her body depleted. He grinned. Nothing had changed with their physical connection; they were still as intensely passionate as they ever were. He laughed. Keona hadn't changed at all, to his delight. From the day they met, she'd put up a guard, wrapped her sweetness in a hard shell; it was why he'd nicknamed her Lollipop. You had to work for her, but it was worth it because once you reached her juicy center, her sweetness rained down nonstop.

Easy stood up on wobbly legs and headed into the bathroom, coming out with a damp cloth. He cleaned Keona and himself and put her in the bed properly before snuggling up with her and closing his eyes to sleep too. His next task was dealing with The Wolf. His Lollipop and their baby boy were home, and Easy would do anything to make sure it was permanent. He was under no illusion things would be perfect, but as long as he and Keona talked more about their separation and made a real effort to rebuild trust, their family would be okay.

Morning came and Elliott was up before the sun, knowing he only had a small window of time to make Keona come before their son was up. He untangled himself from the warmth of her body and used the bathroom, washing his face and brushing his teeth. Then he went back into the bedroom and stared down at his wonderful lover. Keona was on her stomach, her clouds of hair spilling over the pillow, her round ass and the folds of her back calling to him. She was so beautiful and sexy, and he ached to touch her.

Elliott pulled back the covers, moving down between Keona's splayed legs. He lifted her enough to get his face lined up with her pussy and slid his tongue along the lips, licking her and tasting her overnight sweetness. Parting her lower lips, he drenched his tongue in her valley, finding her clit and swirling his tongue around it. Keona started squirming against his face and moaning in her sleep. Easy kept going, moaning into her pussy, loving her taste. His tongue moved over her, catching her creaminess, sliding in and out. It had been two years since he licked the gushy center of his Lollipop; he refused to wait another second.

"Elliott..." Keona whined, and Easy guessed she'd finally realized she wasn't dreaming. A sharp gasp and she was coming, stuttering and moaning, her hand reaching behind her to push his head away. Easy caught the hand in one of his and kept licking, slurping the wetness of her release, going for orgasm #2. Keona bucked against his face, gliding on his tongue, and Elliott loved how she picked up his rhythm. It was as if they'd never been apart.

"Oh, baby, oh, fuck— Elliott, please," she begged him, but he wouldn't let up. He was drowning in her scent and taste and all he wanted to do was taste her. He lapped at her clit then pulled the swollen bud between his lips, swiping it with his tongue while his jaws worked in a gentle sucking rhythm. She lost control then, her orgasm explosive, her body shaking, her face in the pillow to quiet her desperate moans of his name. Easy licked her clean, then finally moved up beside her. Keona burrowed into his arms, whimpering and grabbing for him. He held her tightly.

"Good morning," he whispered. Keona wrapped her thighs around him.

"Good morning yourself, you insatiable man. It's still dark, Elliott; what time is it?"

"Almost time for EJ to be waking up. I had to give my Lollipop some attention before we have to focus on Baby Boy," he said, rubbing her back. Keona laughed.

"You really do think of everything," she said. They dozed together, content to be in each other's arms. The sun peeked over the horizon as they drifted in and out of sleep.

Soon they were up again, welcoming the day. Another quick shower and they were in EJ's room when he opened his eyes. The boy fell into his mother's arms first, grabbing for her shirt. Keona freed her breast and gave it to him, kissing his forehead and wiping his brow.

"Key, what you think about only nursing him when he needs to sleep? I think it will help the two of you pull back some," Easy said, taking EJ's clothes from his bag and arranging them in the closet. He didn't want to rush Keona or be insensitive to her nursing plan, but she'd admitted herself she'd been trying to wean him and not fully committed. Easy didn't want her to start feeling like a milk-producing machine instead of a mom, and he especially didn't want to tire her out too badly. Keona nodded.

"I think it will too. It's a good idea, baby. Tomorrow, I'll just let you give him breakfast like you did yesterday. He was okay, right?"

"Yes, love. He did fine, and he's a good eater. I'm not trying to push you too hard, Key. I only want—"

"I know, Elliott. I can read your cues too, you know. I know you're thinking of me, wanting me to be comfortable and feel secure enough to start letting EJ grow up like he needs to. And you're right because I haven't been as committed to weaning him as I said."

"I'll make us all something good when we get downstairs. Key, does EJ have anything more than these few pajamas and lounging clothes? I thought I got everything out of your car—"

"No, you did," Keona said, her eyes dropping in shame. "He doesn't have anything else. We weren't allowed to go anywhere, so my father never bothered. If it weren't for his housekeeper bringing me hand-me-downs and donations from her church, he wouldn't even have these clothes or a car seat."

"Say no more, baby," Easy said, coming back over to her and sitting on the floor next to her and EJ. "It's okay, babe. We can fix y'all right up today. And lift your head. You're not responsible for him acting like a bitch toward his own grandson. I already saw what you brought for yourself. After I meet with Truck and King, we'll get you and EJ situated."

"Dada really does think of everything, doesn't he, baby?" she whispered to their son, who was finally finished. She scooped him up and patted his back. He burped loudly and then pushed away, wanting his father. Elliott took him, standing up with him and reaching a hand down to help Keona.

"Time for breakfast, family," he declared, and they all went downstairs.

Hours later, Easy finished his meeting with Romelo and Trevino about their next steps. They'd decided to have Bashir close his boxing gym for a few days and send his two managers, Linc and Bunky, to spy on the Wolf's compound and let them know what was going on and when he returned. Trevino chose them because he thought Keona's father would recognize their men. Bash agreed with no hesitation and Linc and Bunky hit the road. Then they strategized on a plan of attack and had a full staff meeting with the team to talk about assignments. Romelo wanted an extra man on Easy's house and with them when they were out, just in case. Easy resisted; he could protect his own family. But Trevino pushed back, told him a backup would allow him to focus more on being with them and adjusting as a new family. Easy gave in, acknowledging the point.

After the meeting, he took his family shopping. He bought clothes and sneakers for EJ and Keona, making sure they had enough to start filling their closets. Then they had a late lunch at a Mexican place they used to love going to together and even got EJ to try a churro. Now they were back home, baby boy had been nursed into a much-needed nap and was asleep in his playpen, and Keona was tidying the living room, spraying fabric refresher on the chairs, dusting the tables and lamps, running their carpet sweeper over the rug, and wiping down EJ's toys before piling them neatly into a small box and sitting it in the corner. Easy sat down on the couch, watching her and immediately aching for her.

"Come sit down, Key. It looks fine," he told her.

Keona waved him off and continued her tidying. "Let me finish dusting."

Easy smirked and opened his jeans, pushing them down along with his boxer briefs and grabbing his dick. He stroked himself to full hardness, anxious to be inside her.

"What if I had something for you to sit on?" he asked, his voice getting deeper. Keona turned, stopping short when she saw him touching himself.

"Oh my," she whispered, licking her lips. Easy smirked.

"Like I said, come sit down," he told her. Keona pushed down her pants and underwear, stepping out of them and walking over. She straddled his lap, sinking down, her pussy gloving his dick and squeezing tightly. They moaned.

"Oh shit, Elliott. Oh shit—"

"Now if you wake the boy, we're gonna have to stop and be Mommy and Daddy again. Can you be quiet for me?" Easy whispered, keeping one eye on the playpen while Keona started to ride him. Her pussy was so tight, so fucking perfect, he could live inside her.

Keona nodded, her hips getting a rhythm. "Yes, I can be quiet, Daddy."

"That's a good Mommy," Easy praised her and held her hips, guiding her up and down. She rode him hard, her mouth open and her head thrown back. Easy had never seen anything more beautiful than Keona and knew he never would. She cried out softly whenever he was buried deep and whimpered in frustration when he glided out. Easy loved her noises, loved how wet she was, how perfectly her pussy wrapped around him. This was his dream, his fantasy...his forever lover. He bit his lip, trying to hold back his own moans while his hands moved to squeeze Keona's soft ass. He used his hips to push up into her as she slid down and her breath hitched, releasing on a breathless whine.

"Fill me up, Elliott. Oh baby," she murmured, trying to be quiet. Easy smiled and stared at her love faces, his pleasure increasing as her wet pussy pulsed around him. She was perfect...and she was home.

Easy watched Keona get closer to her peak, her skin flushed and warm, her body quivering with the need to come. Her beautifully large titties bounced in his face, and he lifted her shirt, catching a nipple in his mouth and suckling her gently. Keona moaned like she couldn't help herself.

"More," she pleaded, never stopping her ride. Easy licked her nipple, swirling his tongue around the dark areola and pulling half her breast into his mouth. He sucked at her nipple harder and felt a gentle squirt of something warm and sweet hit his tongue. He sucked again, hard, getting another stream of her milk and making her moan louder. Easy smiled. She tasted good everywhere.

"Come for me, Lollipop," he ordered, knowing they were both nearly there. After another hard suck of Keona's beautiful nipple and a final gush of her delicious nourishment, he let go and leaned up to kiss her mouth, catching her strangled scream as she came all over him, shaking with the force of her orgasm, her pussy gripping him over and over. Easy followed her, pumping her full of his nut and swirling his tongue around in her mouth. Keona wrenched her lips away and took a deep, gasping breath, looking over her shoulder at the playpen. EJ was still fast asleep. She turned back to Easy, biting her lip.

"You are so bad," she said. "What if our baby had caught us?"

"Then we'd simply have to explain this is how Mommy and Daddy make a sibling, and he needs to get off the titty to make room for them," Easy shrugged. Keona burst into laughter, hitting his chest.

Keona

"Are you sure you want to talk to her? Because the shade she threw when you went to the house was very unnecessary," Nasima asked Keona a couple of days later as the two of them and Sadie walked into the bar Laney managed. Since Keona was committed to staying put this time, she felt like she should try and smooth things over with her old friend. She sighed.

"I have to try at least, Nas. She was a good friend to me, and I abandoned her the same way I did Elliott and everyone else. Her speaking out of hurt is to be expected. And it doesn't matter if she forgives me or not; the point is for me to know I tried to make it better. I can't keep running away from shit when it's hard."

"You're so mature, Key. Is it motherhood?" Sadie said with a grin. The three of them laughed.

"Partly. It was a combination of losing my man and seeing his face in my son every damn day. If I want the life I had—and I do—I have to learn how to fight. And set an example for my baby," Keona replied. She gestured to her two friends to sit at a table while she walked up to the bar where Laney was wiping glasses and sat on a stool. Laney Childs was a beautiful woman with delicate features, deep brown skin, and startling gray eyes, slender but curvy, with her hair in a shoulder-length bob. Once upon a time, she and Keona had been inseparable.

"Hey, Laney. Can we talk?"

"You can say whatever you need to, Keona. Can't promise I'll have anything to say back," Laney replied, rolling her eyes.

Keona took a deep breath. She could handle the attitude. She expected it.

"Laney...look, I'm sorry. I know the way I left was sudden and hurtful. I was in trouble, and I was scared. I thought I had to leave to keep my family safe. I didn't mean for it to happen. But it did, and I hurt you when that was the last thing I wanted to do. We were so tight, you and me, and while I know things can't go back to the way they were, I was hoping you could at least—"

"It's fine, Keona. It happened, and I moved on. Yeah, I missed you and I wondered what was going on, but when I didn't get any answers, I got past it. I don't think we can be cool again, but I'm not mad. Let's agree to let it go," Laney interrupted and said her piece, throwing down her towel and grabbing a tray. Keona was sad as she watched her. A small part of her was hoping Laney would let her explain, let her try to make things better. She sighed.

"Okay, I will respect your wishes. Can my girls and I get three glasses of Pinot Noir when you get a minute?" she said. Laney nodded shortly, and Keona walked away. When she got to the table she sat down, shaking her head and wiping a stray tear.

"I'm sorry, baby. But it'll be okay." Nasima soothed her, patting her back.

Sadie nodded. "We got you, always. And who knows? Maybe she'll come around."

Keona nodded, hoping so. A few minutes later, a server appeared with their wine on a tray. The ladies sipped, Keona savoring her glass since she'd only be able to have one. Having her family around and being able to relax with the ladies was another good reason to wean. She'd like to enjoy more than one glass of wine.

The three of them ordered a few appetizers and talked about life, love, and their incredible men. After about thirty minutes, the bar filled up with more people and two more bartenders came on duty, leaving Laney free to take a break and chop it up with her own friends. They were at a table not too far from Keona, Nasima, and Sadie, and the more they drank, the more their gazes shifted over to stare at Keona and roll their eyes. Keona was committed to ignoring it, knowing they were trying to make her act up and determined not to give them the satisfaction. One of the women stood up, giggling and heading to the bathroom. When she went by their table, she smirked at Keona.

"You'll be gone again soon, and we'll make sure Easy gets over you this time," she said nastily and teetered away. The rest of the women at the table laughed, even Laney. Keona stood up, preparing to let these hags know her man was off-limits. She remembered doing something similar years ago when she first hooked up with Elliott. He had a fan club back then as well, and she had to make it clear she wasn't the one or the two. It seemed some things never changed.

"Laney, I approached you like an adult. You could have said whatever you needed to then. Why are you doing this now? When you know I don't play about Elliott and never have?"

"Keona, me and my girls are over here making conversation. It's not our fault you left your position open," Laney said with a laugh.

Keona laughed too. "I did. And nobody was able to fill it. Ain't that some shit?"

There was a moment of quiet while the women looked away awkwardly. Sadie burst into giggles and Nasima followed. Laney sucked her teeth and waved her hands, attempting to look nonchalant. Keona shook her head and sat down again.

"Whatever, Keona. Ain't nobody thinking about you or Easy."

"You know, lying like this when Sadie and I have seen you offer Easy free drinks and hang on his every word is wild," Nasima added. "Running to feed him info whenever someone he's looking for walks in here. You literally turned yourself into a snitch for him."

"And for nothing. Because you never had a chance, baby girl. We could have saved you some trouble. Easy's heart belongs to one woman—this woman," Sadie said, pointing at Keona. Laney huffed in annoyance and turned her chair.

"That's the real reason you won't forgive me, isn't it? You're not mad I left. You're mad I came back and interrupted your little campaign to make Elliott forget about me," Keona said, surprised at the realization. Laney scowled but didn't get a chance to answer before her friend came back from the bathroom, swiping on more lip gloss.

"Shouldn't you be packing your bags to run away again?" she said, still trying to cause trouble. Keona hopped up from her chair, grabbed the woman by the collar, and yanked her up, shoving her back so hard she fell onto the floor.

"What me and my man go through is our business. You make sure you keep it cute when you see him—and me," she said, her voice hard. The woman scrambled to her feet, shaking with fear.

"You must be new here. Ain't nobody ever tell you Key will rock your shit about Easy?" Sadie said, cackling.

Keona smiled. Her boldness and willingness to cause a scene made everyone assume she was the only borderline possessive one in her relationship, but Elliott's silence was deadly, and she knew without a doubt he'd lay someone out behind her. In her mind, she was matching his energy—only louder.

"Y'all gon have to leave with all this bullshit, Keona," Laney said, helping her friend fix her clothing.

"And who was it who started the bullshit?" Nasima demanded.

"Don't even worry about it, Nas. We'll gladly leave." Keona laughed. "Anybody else want to make a joke about my man before I go?"

Nasima and Sadie stood up. Sadie dropped some bills on the table as she laughed hysterically. Keona smirked. She knew Sadie would encourage her; she was always down to wreck some shit.

"It wasn't that fucking serious. Easy ain't even fine enough for all this," one of the other women mumbled.

"Now you're just lying. Please don't play in my nigga's face and keep his name out your mouth before I throw *your* ass across the room."

"Dammit, Lollipop. You promised me no fighting," Elliott said, walking in with Romelo and Trevino behind him. Keona whirled around, ready to defend herself. She knew her protective detail had called her baby daddy and told him what was happening.

"But she said—"

"Way too much," Sadie finished. "She and her friends were talking mad shit like I won't burn this bitch down with them in it."

After Sadie spoke, the women at the table sat there, mouths open. Laney looked scared. She knew Sadie didn't make idle threats.

"Shug," Romelo said, "we don't threaten people's lives and property because we're mad at them. We talked about this."

"You never let me do anything!" Sadie said, stomping her foot.

Trevino laughed. "Yo, it's time to go. Y'all about to corrupt my Lil Baby," he said.

"Nas don't need us to corrupt her. She was ready to whoop some ass with us," Keona said. Nasima shrugged, going into Trevino's arms and kissing him. Elliott tugged on Keona's top, bringing her over to him.

"Calm down," he whispered and kissed her lips. Keona sighed, leaning into the kiss, feeling her entire body warm up.

Romelo had his face buried in Sadie's neck, rubbing her bottom and swaying back and forth. Keona knew he was calming her. But it was nice to know the ladies had her back.

"Where's EJ?" she asked, pulling back to stare in her man's face. Elliott laughed.

"Oh, now you care where our son is? I know you've been worried about how exposed he is and how many people see him, so he's outside in the car with Bash," he replied.

"Son?" Laney said, her face cracking. Keona shook her head.

"I would have told you if you hadn't given me so much attitude at the bar. But yes, I had Elliott's son and will be having the rest of his children. Still think you got a shot?" she said. Elliott shook his head and pulled her from the bar, Trevino and Romelo following with their significant others.

Outside, Bash and EJ were engaged in a heavy conversation as the baby sat on the hood of the car and Bashir stood in front of him. Bash was fully engaged in EJ's baby talk, nodding his head and answering EJ's half-formed questions. Keona smiled. He and Trevino were going to make great fathers. Knowing both her own history and Nasima's, she was happy their children would have a different life.

"Mama!" EJ yelled out, waving his little hands at her. Keona smiled. Bashir scooped him up and turned, watching them approach.

"What y'all do?" he said, noticing everyone's faces.

"Nothing! They started it!" Keona insisted. Bash laughed. She took her son from his arms and nuzzled his neck. "Hey, Mama's baby," she whispered to him. EJ giggled. As soon as Bash was free, Nas went from Trevino's arms to his, rubbing his beard with her hands. Keona smiled at their easy affection.

"Man, we walked in just in time. The three of them were about to set the whole place off and then let Sadie burn it down," Elliott said, shaking his head.

"We were planning dinner at a nice restaurant. Can y'all put your thug away for a couple of hours?" Romelo asked, amusement in his voice. Sadie assured her for all his bluster, he loved when her hot temper got the best of her. No one was better at handling it than he was.

Sadie smiled. "As long as they don't disrespect my family, I'm good," she said.

"I don't know if EJ can handle anything too fancy. He doesn't sit still very well," Keona said, making an excuse. She could feel the fear creeping back in at the idea of having EJ among strangers and out in the open. Elliott pulled the two of them close, kissing the top of her head.

"Key," he said, using the soft, patient voice he usually reserved for EJ, "it's time to stop hiding him, baby. I know you're scared. I know you've been scared. But we have to let him out into the world—both of you deserve it. He'll be fine for a couple of hours while we have a family dinner."

"We're with you, Key. You know nothing's getting past me," Trevino said. Keona nodded, taking a deep breath. Her rational mind knew Elliott and Trevino were more than capable of protecting them. But she was so used to holding EJ close, and so used to the two of them having only each other. It was going to take some time for the fear to fully recede. But for her amazing baby daddy, she would try.

"Okay," she agreed. "Let's go."

The eight of them piled into two cars and went to a Creole restaurant. Elliott mashed up a salmon filet into a small bowl of rice and beans, and EJ ate the entire bowl and a couple of bites of grits from her shrimp and grits. He drank water and a little juice and was a bit excited but mostly well-behaved. Keona knew after a bowel movement, a bath, and a little nursing, he'd sleep soundly. Dinner was delicious and lively. The conversation flowed, and everyone was at ease. It was almost enough to make Keona forget about her father and the situation she'd run away from. But only almost.

Linc and Bunky reported all was still quiet at the compound. Mae had made herself scarce, but her father hadn't returned. Romelo had reached out to his contacts, trying to figure out where The Wolf might be making his pickup, so they could gauge when he might return. But for the moment, they had a set plan, and everything was ready for the inevitable fallout of him discovering Keona and EJ were gone. Keona tried not to dwell on it, tried to trust Elliott could handle things and that she'd helped all she could by giving him all the information she had.

"Get out of your head, Lollipop," Elliott whispered in her ear. "We got this. You and our son are safe. And I will make sure you stay safe."

"I love you, Elliott," Keona whispered back, unable to help herself. This man was a miracle, always knowing what she needed and when she needed it.

"I love you too, Keona."

After dinner, everyone ended up at Bashir, Trevino, and Nasima's place, playing cards and sharing dessert. Nas was taking a French pastry class, so she invited them to sample fresh baked cream puffs and macarons with homemade raspberry jam. Keona had never tasted anything so wonderful, and she asked about the class, thinking she might like to take it.

"It sounds fun. Maybe after...you know," she said to Elliott as they drove home. She'd been able to find a quiet corner to nurse at Nasima's house, so EJ was sound asleep after a full day. Elliott nodded.

"Baby, don't be afraid to make plans. If you want to wait until we neutralize your dad, then we'll wait. But you can dream as big as you want. I will make anything happen. All you have to do is say the word."

"You're so good to me, Elliott Tanner."

"Who else can I be good to if not the love of my life? You and EJ are my whole world. Plus, I love hearing you talk about doing things to make yourself happy. Hell, you can even bring back your business idea if you want," he said. Keona lit up with happiness that he remembered.

Her degree was in Human Resources, and she'd spent years as a contracts and compensation specialist with a hospital group. Right before her father appeared and she left, she'd mentioned to Elliott she wanted to start her own business doing part-time freelance HR consulting, so they could start their family and she could be home with their children.

"You remember?"

"Baby, of course, I do. And I'd love to see you make it happen. But you know what that means, don't you?" he said, pulling onto the driveway and pressing the button to open the garage. Keona turned her body, looking at his handsome profile as he eased his car next to hers.

"What does it mean?" she asked. Elliott turned off the car, turning to her. He glanced at the backseat.

"It means letting up your hold on EJ, or at least thinking about it. Taking classes, starting your business—both of those means you'll have to trust him with someone, like MomMom, or even eventually a daycare. I know how big that is, and I'm proud of you for relaxing enough to even have those kinds of thoughts," he said. Keona smiled a little. Hearing Elliott say he was proud of her made her warm inside. Her man was a dream come true—always, and in all ways.

The two of them headed into the house with EJ. They put him in bed without even changing him into his pajamas; neither of them wanted to risk waking him.

"Meet me in our room," Keona said and headed downstairs. She fixed a bourbon and soda for Elliott, and one with iced tea for herself. She hadn't had a drink at dinner, and since she was limiting her nursing to naptime and bedtime, she felt comfortable having another one, knowing she wouldn't be nursing until it was time for EJ's nap the next afternoon. Keona took their drinks back up to the bedroom. Elliott was in the shower. She knew he was expecting her to join him, but she was a little hesitant.

Being back home was a sweet and loving dream, but she knew she and her man had more talking to do. Elliott was usually content to stay quiet, but lately he'd been expressing his feelings, and Keona could tell by his looks and touches there was more he needed to say. She had a feeling about what it was. She'd broken his trust when she walked out on him, and he'd missed his son's life because of it. Keona knew there was grace for her because she'd been threatened, but her need to protect clashed with Elliott's trust in her and choosing the former was the wrong decision. There was no impending threat, no monster in the dark she and Elliott couldn't beat together. She knew that now.

Two years in her father's house and under his cruel thumb had opened her eyes to how Keona viewed herself because of him. His early abandonment made her afraid of completely giving her heart, made her feel she was unworthy of staying for. She'd projected those feelings onto Elliott, convincing herself if he knew all her baggage, he'd think it was too much for him. When her father reappeared with his threats, it was easier for her to abandon Elliott by rationalizing that she was protecting him. But deep down, she was also afraid her problems would be too big for him and he wouldn't think she was worth the trouble. Keona knew that was wrong too. There was no one more set on her than her Elliott, no one more suited to her heart. She owed him the same reassurance.

"I was waiting for you, Lollipop," Elliott said, coming out of the bathroom naked and dripping, towel in hand. Keona licked her lips, blowing out her breath. Elliott Tanner was wonderfully made, his semi-hard dick swaying back and forth, almost ready for her. She smiled.

"I'll only be a few minutes," she promised, skirting past him before her lust had her dropping to her knees in front of him.

A quick shower and Keona was back in the bedroom again, wiping water from her body with a fluffy towel. Elliott was under the sheets, enjoying his drink, still naked, flipping channels on the TV. Keona moisturized her body, feeling his eyes on her the entire time. Then she went into their closet, first digging out her locket and putting it back around her neck, then getting a locked box from a drawer in the far corner. She knew Elliott had been curious about the box when he unpacked her things, but he didn't tamper with it or even ask her about it. He'd been waiting for her to trust him.

Keona got into bed with the box. She settled under the blankets, snuggling up to her man, then took his hand. Elliott turned to look at her, his eyes widening when he saw the locket and necklace he'd given her long ago.

"I want you to know I'm here to stay this time," she started, her voice shaky. "Two years ago, I was afraid, and I felt like I had no choice. My father abandoning me, then only coming back when he wanted to use me made me think of myself as someone not worth sticking around for. It was less about not trusting you and more about me feeling like I wouldn't be worth the trouble, Elliott. You have to know that, baby. I need to say it to you. Because I know you've wondered whether you could have done something different, made me open up more. And you couldn't have. It wasn't about you, baby. It was my father's cruelty, and my insecurity."

"Key—"

"I have so much to make up to you as a father. My heart has been on hold for you, Elliott. You haven't missed a thing with me, but you've missed everything with him, and I know you feel it every time you look into his eyes. I can't give you the time back, but maybe I can make it better," Keona said. She used a key on the charm bracelet she wore to open the box and took out two books. She handed them to Elliott, her heart beating fast.

"What are these?" he asked, taking them from her. Keona sighed and gave him a shaky smile.

"My birth journey and EJ's life. The smaller one is a journal where I wrote down my feelings from the day I found out I was pregnant up until he was six months old. I wrote about you, about us, about how I wished with all my heart we were taking the journey together. The second one is a scrapbook. It has EJ's hand and footprints, ultrasound photos, pieces of his clothing, and every milestone I could think of. There's a flash drive. It has video of his first steps and his first words."

Elliott opened one of the books. "It says this book belongs to...me."

"Because it does. I know this doesn't make up for not being there, but I did this for you. I knew I'd be able to give them to you one day. I wanted you to have something that was for you and EJ. I wanted you to know how much we love you. And I hope this reassures you I always planned to find my way home," Keona explained. Elliott started turning the pages, reading her journal entries, running his hands over the pictures in the scrapbook. His breaths sped up, and he looked like he wanted to cry.

"You were all alone, baby. You were alone, and I couldn't help you. He was hurting you, and I—"

"But you're here now, and we're fine. EJ and I are okay," Keona insisted, leaning into Elliott more, interrupting his guilt. She was sick of the blame. All she wanted was her family, strong and together.

"I wished for you." Elliott's voice was shaky as he turned more pages in the scrapbook. "I should have come after you. I should have—"

"I didn't want you to, baby," Keona cut him off, snuggling closer. "He told me he would hurt you, and I believed him. So, when I left, I tried to cut deep with my words, to hurt you so badly you wouldn't even think of coming after me. I didn't mean those things I said when I left, Elliott. I promise you, I didn't mean any of it."

"I know, Key. I know you didn't mean it." Elliott moved the books off his lap and turned, smashing his mouth to hers. Keona kissed him back, felt the wetness of his tears, and began to cry herself. She had to heal her man's heart, by any means necessary. Their two years apart only solidified their need for each other. They had a love that would never die, and Keona was determined to be with him as long as there was breath in her body. She threw her arms around his neck and laid back on the bed, bringing him on top of her. Their tongues wrapped around each other, Elliott rubbed against her, and she moaned.

"Love me, baby. Love me and don't ever stop," she begged breathlessly. Elliott kissed her over and over, sucking on her lips and dragging his tongue over her chin and neck.

"I'll give you everything I have, Lollipop. It's all for you," he promised. He sat up suddenly, bringing Keona with him and putting her thick ass right over his lap. He slapped her soft bottom and moved to her breast, suckling her until she cried out and her milk squirted onto his tongue. She rubbed against his dick, her arousal wetting his lap. The friction stimulated her clit, and she rubbed harder, heading for paradise while Elliott teased her nipples and drank from her.

"Oh, oh, ooh yes," Keona moaned, nearly there. Elliott helped her, pulling her closer, making sure his dick pushed against her swollen clit and rubbed her exactly right. Keona came, gasping for breath, digging her nails into his shoulders. Her climax barely crested before Elliott lifted her, sliding her onto his dick and filling her completely.

"Fuck," he bit out, the contractions of her still-orgasming body gripping him. Keona rode her man fast, her eyes shutting as the pleasure spun her away. His thick length touched her spot as he stroked her from below, and she was delirious.

"Elliott," she whined, her thighs tightening from the exertion. She'd be sore in the morning, but there was no way she wasn't going to ride her man's dick until it was soft every chance she got. She was finally home.

"I'm right here, Lollipop. You got me, baby. You're home to stay, love. Welcome home," he said back, slapping her ass and drinking from her nipples again. Keona whimpered, his words and lovemaking giving her goosebumps. She was spiraling, the pleasure almost overwhelming, her entire body flushed and hot. Elliott thrust upward harder, his head tilting back—a sign he was close. Keona wailed, her climax explosive, her pussy gripping her man's lengthy dick like a vice. He moaned loudly, digging his fingers into her ass, his warm cum spurting into her. Keona's head fell onto his shoulder, her body shaking with aftershocks. Elliott rubbed her back, then her thighs, soothing her body and whispering his love in her ear. When she finally climbed off his lap, he turned to her, smiling. He reached out, pulling on her necklace.

"I can't believe you kept this," he said, his eyes misty with emotion again. Keona nodded.

"I had it with me, but my father took it—he used it to remind me he could hurt you. When I left, I made sure to take it back, to remind me what I was going home to. The last two years have been shaky and scary, Elliott. My whole life was uncertain. There was no way I wasn't coming back to where the ground was solid and steady. There was no way I wasn't coming home to you."

5

Chapter Five

E^{asy}

When the call finally came, Easy was ready. Two nights after Keona showed him the journal and her scrapbook of their son's birth and development, Linc and Bunky reported back to Truck that the Wolf had returned home, and he'd immediately called in his crew. They said the compound was buzzing, and the Wolf was hysterical, desperate to find his daughter and grandson. And to make matters worse, his housekeeper was missing as well. Truck had her in one of Romelo's safe houses with her only living relative—a cousin—so the Wolf couldn't find her and use her for information on Keona. Romelo assigned some soldiers to the outside perimeter and pulled Linc and Bunky home. They were the best at surveillance, but this next part was more than he would ask of them. They had their own lives and deserved to get back to them.

Easy spent the hours leading up to departure with his family, soaking up every minute of them. He insisted on putting EJ down by himself after Key nursed him, promising his son he'd be back home soon and he'd never leave again. Then he went into his bedroom and ravaged Keona, putting all his energy into fucking her senseless and bending her body to his will until she cried, her body so weak she could barely continue to orgasm. He poured every bit of his love into her and filled her with his seed.

"He's gonna pay for hurting you, for taking you away from me. You hear me, Lollipop? I will make him regret everything he put my family through. And then I will come home to you," he promised in a savage whisper as he stroked deep inside her. Keona sobbed, her pussy clenching and convulsing around him, her voice hoarse from calling his name.

"Yes, baby. Please come home," she begged him. Easy continued moving inside her, leaning down to completely cover her and bury his face in her neck. He bit her there, marking her, and then moved down to her beautiful breasts. Suckling her, her sweet milk coating his tongue, Elliott drank from her as he fucked her, feeling like he was nourishing his heart. Keona whimpered, clawed at him, begging for more and for mercy at the same time.

"You and my son will never leave our home again, you understand me? You don't have to be afraid anymore, baby. Daddy's gonna fix it."

"Elliott, I love you," she wailed, her thighs shaking as he pounded into her. Easy didn't let up, didn't stop. He needed this woman to know she was the only one who could make him feel like this. Keona gasped, wet them both with her release, and dug her nails into his arms. Her eyes closed as she came yet again and Easy let her pleasure wash over him. He kissed her soft mouth, licked her tears, calmed her quivering body. He pulled out and moved to Keona's side, gathering her close. Easy heard her soft snores moments later.

Mission accomplished. His alarm was set to wake him in two hours; she'd be sleeping too deep to remember him leaving.

Hours later, Easy arrived at the top of a hill, looking down on Kenyon Ross's estate. He used his phone to check the cameras at his house, making sure Keona and EJ were guarded and safe. Bash would be there soon with Nasima to take everyone to Romelo's house where it was even more secure.

All was quiet at the Wolf's compound, but he could see there were more guards than the usual two Keona had told him about. He was in a nondescript SUV with two of their top lieutenants and another car behind him with four of their most promising soldiers. These boys had military training and an appetite for destruction. Truck was at the back of the compound with their other two lieutenants and extra artillery for any emergencies. The smaller east side gate Keona told them about was covered by four more soldiers and Romelo, who insisted on being a part of this. They'd been dealing with the Wolf's games for a long time, and King wanted him to know the full strength of his might.

Easy powered down the window and leaned out, aiming Truck's beloved grenade launcher at the guard stand and front gate. It seemed like an extreme weapon to use, but they needed the Wolf to know this was a takeover, and anyone who didn't give in would be taken down.

"Be careful with my baby, Easy," Truck's voice came through the earpiece. Easy chuckled. This nigga was as protective of his weapons as he was of Nas and Bash.

"Ain't nothing gon happen to your shit, nigga."

"If it does, you know Sadie can get you another one," Romelo jumped into the conversation. Besides being his love, Sadie was their equipment specialist, sourcing everything from weapons and ammo to communications mics, burner phones, signal jammers, and tactical gear.

"Fat Mama is already calibrated exactly the way I want her; I don't want to have to start again."

"Nas know you call your grenade launcher the same name you call her?" Romelo asked. Easy laughed. Like Key, Nasima was a beautiful, plump woman, and Truck and Bash usually referred to her as "Lil Baby" or their "pretty fat mama."

"She know who was first. I named it Fat Mama because I missed her. It's like a dedication to her," Truck insisted, and everyone burst into laughter.

"Worst logic ever, nigga. Anyway, we're a go. Y'all lock in. And remember, everything goes. We reducing this shit to ashes. It's open season, but I got personal business with The Wolf. He's mine," Easy said, peering through the scope. He lined up his aim and pulled the trigger.

The grenade hit its mark, and the guard stand exploded, taking the left side of the gate with it and waking up the compound. Easy stepped on the gas and flew down the hill and onto the Wolf's property. Romelo's crew drove through the flimsy east side gate and Truck came from the back. Their soldiers started shooting out of the windows, picking off the men running out to see what was happening. Everyone gathered at the main house and their crew spilled out of the cars, splitting up as they discussed.

The Wolf's men started pouring out from the main house and the auxiliary houses as gunfire filled the air. Easy dropped low, making his way into the main house with Romelo behind him. They knew Truck would command the troops outside and wouldn't leave a soul alive.

Easy went in the front door, gun raised, with Romelo flanking him. They made their way through the entire downstairs, picking off the four men who stayed behind with ease and precision. Because of Keona, they knew all the house's hiding places and made quick work of tearing them apart. Two of their soldiers entered the house, ready to take anything of value they'd uncovered, and Easy left Romelo with them, making his way upstairs.

When he got to the landing, he headed straight to the huge master suite, knowing where Kenyon Ross was most likely hiding. Keona told them he had a panic room behind his bedroom closet. He entered the room quietly, his silenced weapon putting three bullets into the neck of a soldier who was guarding the bedroom before he could even lift his weapon. Hearing a noise, he turned and saw Truck behind him, his knife bright with the blood of the man he'd seen sneaking up behind Easy. He nodded his head, and Easy nodded back.

The two men went to the closet, heading to the back corner where the entrance to the panic room was. Easy moved the wall mirror the way Keona told him to, and the keypad popped out. Now, to think of what the code might be. It was the only thing Keona didn't know. Truck narrowed his eyes, thinking. Then he looked at Easy.

"Try EJ's birthday," he whispered. Easy blinked, wondering what prompted his friend to think of that. He inputted his son's birthday and the keypad lit up green, the wall parting to reveal a door. Knowing the panic room most likely had weapons and the Wolf would be ready to defend himself, Easy and Truck flanked the door, throwing in a flash bang grenade and closing it. Three seconds later, it went off, and they went in, taking advantage of the smoke and disorientation. They dragged the Wolf out and into the bedroom area, throwing him onto the bed.

Kenyon Ross was coughing and rubbing his eyes, trying to get his bearings. Easy punched him in the mouth, snapping his head back and making him moan. Face to face with the man who'd stolen and abused his family, all Easy could see was red.

"Leave me with him," he said to his best friend. Truck stared at him, his gaze questioning.

"You don't want me to—"

"When it was Smoke and Tone, you needed to be hands off, and I gave it to you," Easy reminded him. "Give me this."

Truck nodded, leaving the room to check on Romelo. Smoke was Nasima's cousin, and Tone her ex-boyfriend. They were two bums who'd taken advantage of Nasima and tried to intimidate her and bleed her dry. All it took was a tear over them and Truck was ready to wipe them off the face of the Earth in defense of his love. But Truck's more violent enforcer persona was hard for Nasima, so when it was time to take them out, he left it to Easy and the team, not wanting to bring that darkness into his home. And Easy understood.

But his situation was different. Keona needed to know the threat was gone and the fear could go with it. She needed to be able to rest, knowing she didn't have to run and no one would come for her ever again. The best way to assure her was eliminating the threat himself. The blood on his hands would be worth it because Keona and EJ's safety would be guaranteed.

"Remember me, Kenyon?" Easy said, punching the man in the jaw again. The Wolf was still rubbing his irritated eyes, trying to get his bearings. He squinted, blinked, and stared at Easy.

"You...my daughter— You—"

"You do remember me," Easy continued, pulling a knife from one of his pockets and some wire from another, setting them aside. Ross hopped up and tried to swing but was knocked back down by the butt of Easy's gun. He yelled in pain, dropping to one knee on the floor. Easy hit him over and over, bludgeoning him with fists of fury until he was curled into a ball on the floor, his blood on the carpet. Easy got down to his level, stared into his eyes.

"You will pay for every moment of pain my wife and son suffered at your hands," he promised, his voice cold. He pressed a button on his phone, and two of their soldiers came into the room.

"Help me tie him up, then empty the panic room," Easy instructed them. The two soldiers did his bidding, using the wire to tie the Wolf's wrists and ankles to a chair in his bedroom. They emptied the panic room of money, weapons, and product and went back downstairs.

"Fuck you!" the Wolf spat out, one eye closed, his lips swollen. "You won't break me."

"I ain't trying to get no information," Easy laughed. "Ain't shit about your operation I need to know. Hell, you don't even have an operation no more. This is an execution, my nigga. You threatened me to put fear in my wife, took her and my son to punish me, and abused them. You didn't even care that they're your family too. I'm about to get it back in blood. Best believe that."

An hour later, Easy had worked out most of the anger he felt knowing what Kenyon Ross had done to his family. The man was dead—his skin sliced open in multiple places and bruised by brass knuckles, his fingers, toes, jaw, and finally, his neck broken. Easy didn't feel triumphant, but he did feel accomplished. When he could lift a burden from Keona, when he could solve a problem for her, he felt like he was succeeding as her man, as her protector—hers and EJ's.

All was quiet in the house and outside, and Easy knew the rest of the crew was finishing the final sweep and clean-up and waiting for him. He pressed another button on his phone, and two soldiers entered the room moments later, gas cans in hand, ready to douse the room.

"You good, Easy?" one of them asked. Easy looked up, startled out of his thoughts. He eyed the man who'd spoken to him, nodding.

"Yeah, Malice," he said, turning to leave the room, "I'm good."

Though it would be hours still before they would leave for home, at least he could rest knowing he'd completed the mission. When he got downstairs, Truck was organizing the dead men's bodies in the living room, and the boys were pouring gasoline on them too. They were much better off setting the whole thing ablaze. The few in the Wolf's crew who hadn't been killed would be given the opportunity to prove their loyalty under Truck and Easy's watchful eye.

"We got a small problem," Romelo said, coming in the front door. Easy turned to face his friend.

"Wassup?"

"One of those auxiliary houses has women, five or six, who were taken from all over the country and sold to the Wolf. I knew the nigga would traffic anything he could, but damn. There should be boundaries on some shit," Romelo said, shaking his head. Easy snorted.

"He upstairs with his neck broke because he don't know the meaning of boundaries. I'm not surprised at all. Key knew there were women, but she said she never saw them. What do you want to do with them?"

"They've been beaten and drugged—half of them don't even know where they are or where they were snatched from. We can't let them go out here. They'll be even more fucked up," Romelo continued.

"We'll take them home," Truck said, coming into the foyer and joining the conversation. "Nas will know what to do. When she was away, she did intake and accounting work for social services organizations. She'll know where we can take them so they'll be safe."

The three of them nodded, and Romelo sent some of their men to get the women ready and settled. The three best friends got into work mode, commanding the clean-up crew and making sure there was no trace of them anywhere. It made them all shift back to the days when they were still on the takeover. These days, with Romelo's territory vast and ruled with an iron fist, they spent most days making sure everything they put in place was running smoothly. Dirty work like this was from the olden days when they were still solidifying who they were in this game.

The Wolf's compound was in a lonely valley, with his closest neighbors over two miles away; those neighbors had been given a mysterious vacation and removed from their home earlier in the week so there were no extra eyes. It was one more thing Truck anticipated, and one more thing they could breathe easier about.

"Hey," Easy called out to his best friend. Truck turned from his work. "How did you figure out the code to his panic room?"

Truck shrugged. "I remembered what Key said about EJ being his real legacy. Figured the nigga would anticipate grooming him, and his ego would have him preparing for EJ to take his throne. It was a calculated guess, but a good one."

Easy nodded and went back to work. Truck was the smartest nigga he knew—he even graduated high school a year early—so it was no shock he was able to put that logic together. The way his mind worked was why Romelo brought him in. Easy took inventory of what had been collected from the Wolf's compound: deeds to the land they were on, papers for miscellaneous assets, some stocks, bonds, jewelry and artwork, thousands of dollars, pounds of product—although Romelo could tell by looking it wasn't the quality of theirs—and a stockpile of weapons, extensive but not nearly enough to defend an entire compound. It seemed the Wolf was barely making it and merely keeping up appearances.

"We're burning the product too," Romelo announced, frowning. "I'm not soiling my good name with it. Our customers would riot if we gave them that bullshit as is, and to make it potent again, we'd have to cut it with something so sharp it'll kill mufuckas, and we can't afford bodies in the street right now. Let that shit burn." Truck laughed at his cousin. King took his reputation seriously, and their product was the best. Easy smiled.

"You got it, boss," he said to Romelo, nodding in acknowledgement and going back to his inventory.

The next morning, Easy entered one of Romelo's guest rooms and slid quietly into bed with his wife and son. He'd stopped at his own home to shower and change and brought his "work clothes" back to Romelo's to throw into his incinerator. He threw his arm around Keona and pulled her against him. She whimpered.

"Elliott," she called his name, still sleeping. He kissed her neck.

"I'm right here, Lollipop," he whispered. "I'm home."

Keona

Keona was having the most wonderful dream. She was dreaming of her baby daddy, wrapping her in his arms and whispering in her ear that he loved her and wanted her to marry him. She snuggled closer, getting his scent in her nose, feeling like he was there.

"Marry me, Lollipop," Elliott was saying, kissing her neck over and over. She moaned, trying to say yes, but his hands running over her body were a distraction.

"Yes. I love you, baby," she thought she whispered back and drifted off again.

When she awoke again, she was alone, the arm she used to cuddle EJ to her empty. She sat up, her eyes widening with fear. She was confused about the room until she remembered she was at Romelo's house for safety. But where was EJ?

"EJ?" she called. "EJ, where are you? Did you get out of bed? Answer Mama."

"I got him, Key," Elliott said from below. Keona gasped and leaned over the bed. Her son and his father were on the floor, running his toy trucks back and forth over the rug. She smiled. Last night wasn't a dream after all.

"Hi, Mama!" EJ greeted her, waving his chubby arms. She waved back, then lifted her arms over her head, yawning and stretching. She got out of bed to head to the bathroom. Elliott hopped up, pulling her into his arms while keeping one eye on their son.

"Gimme kiss. I missed you," he demanded. Keona giggled.

"You need to let me brush my teeth first, sir," she replied. Elliott shook his head.

"I don't care. I went twenty-four hours without my lips on yours—gimme my kisses." Keona wriggled free, covering her mouth and shaking her head. She ducked into the en suite, Elliott's laughter ringing behind her. When she came out, she went right into his arms, smashing her lips against his. Elliott grabbed her bottom in his hands and lifted her against him, kissing her back. They both moaned and her arms went around his neck, holding tight. Keona's heart swelled with joy. Her man was home. The danger was gone. Their son was safe forever, and Elliott wanted to marry her.

"Dada, pway!" EJ yelled, anxious to get his father's attention back. Keona and Elliott split up, laughing, and he went back to the floor. A knock sounded at the door.

"Come in!" Keona called out. The door opened and Nasima poked her head in.

"Good morning, family," she said to them. She hugged Keona and went over to Elliott and EJ, scooping up the baby and the toy he was playing with. EJ squealed with happiness as soon as he was in her arms. She started out of the room without another word.

"Umm… Nas? Where you going?" Elliott asked. Nasima turned back to them with a wink and a smile.

"I got my 'successful mission and we made it home safely' gift this morning. But I figured the couple with the baby needed some alone time so Key can get hers too. We'll be downstairs, having brunch and opening all the presents Sadie and I bought him," she said, leaving the room. The door closed again, and the parents turned to each other, laughing.

"They are a trip," Keona said, "and they're spoiling him."

"They making up for lost time, which our son deserves. And truth be told, I was trying to entertain him into an early nap so I could get a hold of you," Elliott replied.

Keona laughed, hopping back onto the bed and beckoning to him. Elliott followed, tackling her and settling between her thighs. They kissed again, soft, wet kisses full of love and desire. Keona couldn't believe these lips were hers again; she got to feel them on her mouth and body, and she got to listen to the love flowing from between them. The time she'd spent without Elliott was still a pain pulsing through her veins, a dull ache she feared would never go away.

"It's us from here on out, Key," Elliott whispered between kisses. "You can relax, love. No one is taking you and EJ from me again." Keona gasped, her heart catching. Tears fell from her eyes. How did he always know what she needed to hear?

"I love you, Elliott," she said. He smiled, leaning up and tugging at the T-shirt she was wearing. Keona clawed at his clothes, anxious to feel his body against hers. Soon they were chest to chest, tongues and lips smacking against each other. Elliott growled deep in his throat as his mouth moved with hers. His hands gripped the sides of her belly and caressed her hips, his thumbs dipping into the curve of her waist. Keona rubbed herself against him, running her fingers over his shoulders and neck. Elliott grunted into her mouth, letting her know her touch felt good to him. He moved to the side slightly and his mouth wrapped around her nipple. He sucked hard, and Keona gasped in pleasure. She knew the moment he was sampling her milk because he began to moan and tug her other nipple with his fingers. Keona cried out softly, her pussy getting wetter with every pull of his mouth.

"Fuck, you taste good," Elliott mumbled and went back to suckling her. His hand slid down her body, his touch light, raising goosebumps on her skin. His fingers pushed her panties to the side and parted her pussy lips, swiping over her swollen clit. Keona's body bucked, and she grabbed for her man's ears, rubbing them as she moaned raggedly. Elliott continued playing in her pussy, delving in to fill her with his fingers, then pulling out to rub the wetness on her clit. His mouth kept busy at her nipple and soon, Keona was coming hard, her eyes slamming shut and her mouth opening wide in a breathless cry. Elliott leaned up, pushing off his sweats and boxer briefs before moving down to tug off her panties. He got on top of her, his hard dick teasing her wet opening.

"You miss me, Lollipop?" he asked, staring into her eyes. Keona smiled, still catching her breath a bit. *He's so fine and he's mine,* she thought lovingly.

"Yes, my baby. I missed you so much. My heart can barely take it when I'm away from you now."

"It was for a good cause, though. You're safe, my love. You're safe for good. And so is EJ. We can move on with our lives and our dreams now," he promised. He started easing inside her, stretching her with his thickness. Keona spread her legs wider.

"Thanks to you, Elliott. You saved us, like I knew you would."

"Like I always will," he said, kissing her mouth and sliding his dick fully inside. Keona inhaled and exhaled in a moan. Elliott started moving, thrusting in and out, pumping his hips, finding a snug, wet home over and over. She held onto his shoulders, the pleasure nearly dizzying. He was so hard, so big. She was full and drowning in ecstasy.

"Elliott! Oh baby, I—fuck me!"

"Take this dick and give me my babies. You promised, Key. You promised me," he growled out, stroking harder and deeper, bottoming out in her soaked pussy. Keona came, her body shaking, her head spinning. But Elliott kept going.

"You hear me? You having more of my babies?" he continued. Keona was moaning, her body floating into space. She could barely think. His dick was scattering her brain, stealing her thoughts, making her lose it.

"Keona?"

"Yes, baby, yes!" she screamed, another orgasm crashing through her body. She held onto Elliott tightly, tears sprouting from her eyes. Elliott kept going, fucking her into oblivion, thrusting hard, pounding into her. Keona called his name, dug her nails into his shoulders, drowned in his lust. Her pussy added to the song of her moans, the wetness creating a lush smacking sound that echoed in the room. Elliott was focused, his mouth buried in her neck, his groans muffled but still urgent. He was close. Keona moved her hands up to his neck, rubbing and soothing him with her touch.

"Give me a baby, Daddy," she whispered to him, and they spun away together, coming at the same time, their mutual orgasm shaking the bed and their cries filling the room. Elliott kissed her neck and pulled out, going to her side and pulling her into his arms.

Forty minutes later, the two of them made their way downstairs. In Romelo's massive eat-in kitchen, Sadie sat with EJ on her lap, both enjoying her waffles and fruit while Bashir sat across from them with Nasima in his lap. He was rubbing her plush body with his eyes closed and a soft smile on his face while she munched happily on a bacon, egg, and cheese biscuit.

"Hey! There's plenty. We have breakfast sandwiches, fish and grits, waffles, fruit, scrambled eggs, and bacon," Nasima said with a smile. Keona sat next to Sadie, turning to take EJ off her hands. Sadie waved her away, gesturing to the food on the table.

"Eat. He's fine," she said. Keona grabbed a plate and put two biscuit sandwiches and some fruit onto it.

"Where are Truck and Rome?" Elliott asked.

"In the war room, debriefing. They said for you to make a plate and join them," Bashir relayed. Romelo wasn't a "formal dining" kind of person, so what was originally the dining room was a war room of sorts, a place for them to discuss product placement and changes to the distribution chain, count money, and review territory logistics and upcoming pickups. Elliott nodded, quickly fixing a huge plate of fish and grits and stuffing eggs and bacon on the side. He kissed Keona and EJ and left the kitchen.

"I see you have the 'successful mission and home safe' glow," Sadie said, offering EJ a blueberry. The little boy took it, popping it into his mouth and grinning as he chewed.

"It matches yours," Keona laughed, "and theirs." She pointed to Nasima and Bashir.

"I can confirm Romelo was very happy to see me," Sadie said with a sly grin on her face. Nasima giggled and turned around to kiss Bashir before going back to her sandwich.

"Elliott was a little too happy. The man is a machine. I think I need to go back to sleep," Keona said, taking a bite of her biscuit sandwich.

"We all do," Bashir mumbled, still rubbing on Nasima with his eyes closed. The three women burst into laughter.

Later, Elliott took them home and they spent the rest of the day focused on their son. The two of them organized EJ's room, ordered new things for him, and helped him line up all his new toys and games. His aunties had gone all out for him, buying him everything appropriate for his age. His Uncle Bash was a sneakerhead, so his contribution was new pairs of all the best toddler walking sneakers on the market. They called it a welcome home gift since they never got to give her a baby shower. Keona was in tears staring at it all, and EJ was in heaven.

"I can't believe this," she whispered. Elliott smiled and cuddled her to his side.

"Believe it. He's loved, and so are you. Welcome home, Lollipop," he replied, kissing her tears.

6

Chapter Six

K<u>eona</u>
<u>**Six Weeks Later**</u>

"No bed, Mama. Snack, Mama. Snack!" EJ demanded as Elliott turned onto their street. Keona shook her head as Elliott laughed. This child would chew and swallow while he slept if he could.

"You have had enough to eat, little boy. You can have some water, and then it's bedtime."

"Snack, Dada!" EJ tried his luck with his father. Keona turned to see Elliott shrugging as if he was about to give in, and she scowled at him. He laughed again as he pulled up to their townhouse and onto the driveway. He hit his remote and the garage door began to open.

They were coming from a backyard barbecue at Trevino, Nasima, and Bashir's house. They lived in a lovely Victorian left for Bash by his grandmother and the backyard space was great for entertainment. It was a fun, family-filled day, and everyone had a good time. It prompted conversation between the couple about whether they should move to a place with more outdoor space. The idea intrigued Keona, but she loved their house.

Once the garage door was open, Elliott started to pull in when a car stopped in front of the house. Keona saw him look in his rearview, trying to see if he recognized the person, and when it was clear he didn't, he pulled his gun discreetly and opened his door, motioning for her to stay inside the car.

"Yo, can I help you?" he called out. Keona stayed where she was, removing her seatbelt and unbuckling EJ in case she had to move quickly. Moments later, Elliott came to her door, opening it and reaching in for her.

"Who is it?" she questioned. Elliott sighed.

"Your mother," he answered.

Keona's eyes widened. Kimberly Ross? Here? Why? She got out of the car and started back down the driveway, meeting her mother halfway. Elliott grabbed their son from the car and fol-lowed.

"Mom?"

"Key," her mother said softly.

Kimberly Ross passed on nearly everything physical to her only child—wide body, burnt umber skin, brown hair. They even shared the same small, wide nose and lip shape. But Keona had her fa-ther's eyes. Her mother was dressed expensively as always—de-signer belted shirt dress with a flared skirt, D&G slip-on sneakers, and a Prada handbag, diamonds glittering on her neck, wrists, and ears. Kimberly opened her arms, but Keona didn't go into them. *I know she didn't show up here like everything is cool,* she thought.

"What are you doing here?" she asked instead. Kimberly seemed confused by her daughter's standoffish demeanor and put her arms down, her fists clenching at her sides awkwardly.

"I wanted to—I needed to see the man who put The Wolf down like the rabid dog he was, for one thing. Thank you, Easy. I always knew you would protect her."

"Someone has to," Elliott answered, his face blank but his al-mond-colored eyes bright with suspicion and anger. He held their son to him tighter, and EJ snuggled against his father, silent and observant.

"I suppose that's true," Kimberly said, looking away for a moment. Keona was confused. Her mother threw her to the wolves, one wolf specifically, a long time ago. Why in the world would she show up here now?

"Mom, you didn't answer my question. What are you doing here?" Keona asked again. She sighed and closed her eyes briefly, searching for patience. It seemed like this woman had a sixth sense for when she was happy and made her way to Keona to cause chaos.

Keona and her mother had moved around a bit when she was growing up, allegedly trying to stay out of the Wolf's path. When she was a senior in high school, her mother brought her to the place where she met the love of her life, and Keona wanted to stay. But when she graduated, her mother said it was better to start over somewhere else and not get too comfortable. The two of them went away, and Keona attended college and got a job. She missed Elliott and wished every day she could go back to him, but with her mother hanging over her, it was impossible.

When she was twenty-six, she finally got her chance. Kimberly told her it would be better if they separated for a while, and Keona took her ass home to her man. She was happy, protected, satisfied, and safe and planned on staying that way. But two years ago, every-thing fell apart, and her mother was right in the center of it.

Kimberly bit her lip, suddenly nervous in the face of her daugh-ter's anger. "You're my daughter, and I want to see you. I want to hold my grandson. I want—why are you being so cold to me?"

"Are you serious right now? You really think I would let you back into my life? And let you touch my child? Why are you here,

Kimberly? Because ain't no way you think we're good after the shit you did."

"Your father is— Keona, I'm sorry. I tried to apologize. Everything happened so fast. I didn't know he'd take you—"

"He didn't only take me, Mom! He threatened Elliott and his family! He put me on display for his deviant friends, trying to find someone to sell me to. He stole my baby from his father, and he tried to steal him from me!" Keona shouted, her eyes blurring with tears. Elliott brought her back against him and held her tightly. EJ whined, his sensibilities disturbed from seeing her get upset. His father growled low, and Keona knew he was getting angry. He knew the part her mother played in keeping them apart after high school, how she'd controlled Keona with fear. He wasn't her biggest fan either.

"Kimberly, you need to go. I don't know what you've done now, or what you were hoping to accomplish by coming here—"

"I can tell you what she's done," Keona interrupted Elliott, wiping her eyes. She turned to kiss her baby's cheeks and calm him down. Then she stepped back over toward her mother, keeping a tight hold on Elliott's hand. Kimberly backed away, her breath stuttering as she stared at Keona.

"Two years ago, when the Wolf first came here to find me, she knew. She knew the whole time, Elliott. When he popped up on me with weeks of surveillance, I was losing my mind. I had no idea he'd been watching us for so long. But **she** did. She knew the moment he got here, and she didn't tell me. She didn't *warn* me. You know what she did instead? She fed him information about me. And that's when I found out she'd been doing it for years. Those women my father was trafficking, my mother was finding them for him. She recruited other women so he'd pay for her lifestyle and leave her alone. And when he decided he wanted me, she gave *me* to him too, with no hesitation. My own mother."

"Keona, I'm sorry, baby. I didn't know things would get so out of hand."

"You knew," Elliott interjected quietly. "You simply didn't care because as long as Key was the focus, he left you alone."

"Kenyon was a dangerous man. You don't understand—"

"I still feel his hands going across my face, around my neck. I can still hear his threats to take my baby away and sell me into prostitution. Don't tell me how dangerous he was. You weren't in that house with him."

"You think you're the only person your father ever abused? I have a past too, Keona," Kimberly insisted, getting visibly frustrated. Keona shook her head.

"Wouldn't your past be even more reason to warn me? You knew what kind of man he was and what he could do to me. If I hadn't been pregnant with EJ when he took me, I doubt I would have made it back here," she said. Kimberly Ross blew out her breath, her bottom lip quivering. She looked lost and guilty. Keona sighed. This was all too much for one night. She turned to Elliott, on the verge of tears again. He nodded.

"What is it you want, Kimberly? Even if we were going to let you spend time with our son, appearing at our house in the dark with no advance notice wasn't the way to go about it. I know there's something else. What is it?" Elliott said, taking charge of the conversation. Kimberly swallowed, slinging her handbag over her shoulder again.

"I was— You know Kenyon and I never legally divorced. I wanted to know if my name was on anything you found at the compound."

"You're here for money? How much did he pay you to keep quiet and sell me out two years ago? It couldn't have been much if you've gone through it already. I can't fucking believe this," Keona raged. Elliott pulled her against him again and kissed the top of her head. Then he shifted EJ to his other arm, pushing him into Keona's embrace.

"I disarmed the house. Go ahead inside, I'll be right there," he said softly. Keona looked up into Elliott's eyes, saw his determination and love, and nodded her head. She took their son and turned to walk to the front door.

"Keona, I—please! I'm sorry. I want to make it up to you. I promise I came here for you!" Kimberly yelled, but Keona kept walking. She entered the house and carried EJ up the stairs to the living room, sitting him down with some toys and going into the kitchen with tears running down her face. Keona was hurting inside, her heart clenching, her head pounding. Her life was finally settling into something normal and happy and here was her mother, stirring things up.

Keona understood survival. And she understood abuse. But as a mother herself now, she knew nothing could ever make her intentionally put EJ in harm's way. Why would Kimberly do it to her? She sighed and looked over into the living room to make sure EJ was okay. Then she poured a glass of wine, only to remember she couldn't drink it because she still had to nurse. Her eyes filled with tears again and she let them fall, frustrated and angry. She was still staring at the glass, crying, when Elliott came in a few minutes later.

"Key? What— Aww, baby. Come on, come on now. I got you," he said, pulling her into his arms. She threw her arms around his torso and sobbed, trying to hold back her noises so she wouldn't scare their child.

"Why wouldn't she protect me? I'm her daughter!" she bawled into his shirt. Elliott rocked her and kissed her hair, squeezing her tight.

"She's doing what she knows how, Key—surviving. Your mom's been living scared for a long time, with only survival on her mind. And she's been playing your dad's game and participating in his lifestyle for a long time too. It's enough to mess anybody up. Your loyalties can get pretty twisted when you want to make it from one score to the next."

"Now what? I'm supposed to just forgive her?" Keona leaned back, staring up at him incredulously. It sounded like he was taking her side, making an excuse for her duplicity.

"No, baby, of course not," he hurried to reassure her, frowning at the look in her eyes. "You don't have to if you don't want to, especially since she fumbled by showing up here trying to get something out of you. I told her you'd been living in fear mode too, and you were moving past it, and she bet not even think of showing up here again until she was making moves to get past it too. I made it plain I wasn't sacrificing EJ's safety or your peace for anybody, and she needed to wait until you were ready, no matter how long it took."

"What did she say?"

"She said she had no idea how to earn your trust, but she was willing to wait and to try. Then she said EJ was beautiful and she wished she'd been able to hold him."

"Did you give her money, Elliott?" Keona wanted to know. He shook his head, smirking.

"Nah. I peeped her dress and shoes—Kimberly's used to having a sponsor and ain't no fucking way she getting the kind of money she needs out of us—but she was right. There was paperwork at the compound for a handful of assets your father put in her name.

I told her I'd see Romelo about getting those things back to her. Then she left."

"You think she really wants to try?" Keona asked in a little voice. Elliott kissed her forehead.

"I think if she really does, you'll know. Because she'll prove it to you. And you don't have to decide anything until she does. Come on, Lollipop. Let's get this boy nursed so you can have some wine. You were looking pitiful staring at your glass." His joke at the end made Keona snort with laughter, and she slapped his chest.

"Don't make fun of me," she said. He chuckled and went to the living room to get EJ.

<u>Easy</u>

"Kimberly pulled up on y'all? After all this time?" Romelo asked as Easy sat with his two friends the next day. They were in Romelo's war room, doing the count, remnants of lunch surrounding them. Teddy and Scratch, Romelo's bodyguards, stood at the door. The room was enclosed, soundproofed, and the windows bulletproof, plus there was a passageway behind a painting leading to a tunnel and outside. It was a panic room of sorts, well worth the money Romelo spent to create it, and the safest place to do the weekly count.

"Yup. Rolled up last night, talking about she want to be with her daughter and hold her grandson. Key wasn't going for it. She claimed she felt so bad and she only came for her family. Didn't stop her from wondering whether Kenyon had anything in her name, though," Easy replied, wrapping a stack of bills and putting it to the side for his payment run.

Every individual dealer kept a quarter of what they made from selling, but it was Easy's job to pay everyone who didn't sell directly—hitters, guards, runners, and the guys who ran the stash house. It's part of the reason they called him The Watcher. He had his eye on the money, always. And since he drove around their territory so much doing pickups and drop offs, he had the chance to see a little bit of everything.

Easy had supervised the pickups and re-ups and now they were counting money. Trevino shook his head as he put a stack of bills into the machine and picked up another to count by hand. He always double-checked.

"Tell Key to hold her head. I don't trust Kimberly at all," Trevino finally said, finishing his manual count and adding the new stack to the machine as Romelo removed the one he'd put there before. "I heard rumblings about her 'recruiting' for the Wolf. When Key came home, I started looking into Kimberly more. Turns out, she promised Kenyon she'd bring Key into the fold years ago. And when she had to go back and tell him she was with us, he was even more pissed. He thought Key switched sides, thought she was working for us. Kimberly did tell him she was only your woman and had nothing to do with the operation; I guess he didn't believe her."

"Still pretty fucked-up to plot on your own daughter, but what do you expect? Years of playing Kenyon's games and letting him use you to pimp women would mess anyone up. But he did leave a townhouse in her name, plus some artwork and a couple of vintage cars being stored in a private garage upstate. I'll get in touch, hand the stuff over to her."

"Thanks, Rome. I appreciate it. I'm not really hyped to talk to her again, and I know Keona don't want to. I told her not to come back until she gets a handle on her shit. I'm not gonna have my wife and son unsettled. We getting into a good routine, and they feel safe. I'm not letting anything fuck it up," Easy said, wrapping another stack of bills.

"Nor should you. Key's home, and the Wolf is gone. We got enough to worry about trying to run this shit on the day-to-day. Last thing we need is Kimberly making waves," Trevino added.

"She won't. And I'll make it clear we won't tolerate it when I hand this stuff over to her. Good thing Trevino told me to keep it. He anticipated her resurfacing," Romelo said, nodding at his cousin. Trevino shrugged.

"It's what I do. It's how we survive." He brushed off the praise and went back to his count. Easy got back into his work, making notes and marking amounts down in the ledger. The three of them finished and then had a strategy meeting. After, Trevino went to the warehouse to supervise the new shipment and Romelo went into a roundtable meeting with some new buyers for their weapons stock. Easy left and hit the street, paying their employees and riding through to check on things. It was going to be a late night for him, but his Lollipop was home safe with their baby boy, and they made all the work feel worth it.

Keona

"No bed, Mama! I want Dada!" EJ screwed up his Elliott-looking face and shook his head back and forth. Keona sighed. He'd been fed, bathed, and nursed. And still, she'd been trying to get him to lie down for an hour.

"I want Dada too, but he's working. Please lie down, EJ. Come on, it's bedtime," she coaxed, nudging him down again. She patted his back, hoping the soothing motion would settle him long enough for his eyes to close. She knew he was tired. They'd had a long day while she tried to distract herself from her mother's visit. Breakfast with MomMom, a trip to the park with Auntie Nas, and shopping with Auntie Sadie—this time for groceries, more toys, wall decorations for his room, and storage for his toys in the living room. EJ was still quiet, like his father, but in the weeks since they'd arrived, he'd embraced his new family, home, and surroundings with remarkable speed and adaptability. Keona was more than a little amazed.

If she were being honest with herself, part of her was a bit overwhelmed and jealous. It'd been her and EJ alone for so long. But he was growing socially by leaps and bounds in such a short amount of time—fully content to be held, cuddled, and entertained by people other than her. It was making her feel a little out of sorts...and unneeded. MomMom said it was natural and simply proof it was time for her to get her own life again. Keona knew she was right, but still. Her little baby needing someone other than her stung a little. And it didn't hit harder with anyone than it did with his father.

EJ's complete obsession with Elliott was fascinating, to say the least. The two of them usually woke up together, welcoming the sun while she slept in. Since she'd been forgoing morning nursing, she was much more well-rested. She was grateful and thought it was adorable her boys had their alone time to bond, but it was starting to make her feel useless as a mommy.

Keona sighed. Maybe it was time to get a life. EJ growing and expanding his circle was a good thing, and there was no reason for her to be jealous of it. Especially since Elliott never missed a beat with her. Their love was regaining its strength every day.

EJ twisted out of her hold and sat up again. "Dada!" he demanded, balling his fists. Keona rolled her eyes. *Traitor*, she thought. She stood up and held out her arms for her son.

"How about a snuggle party and TV with Mama?" she said. EJ jumped into her arms, and she carried him into her and Elliott's bedroom, settling them both under the blankets against the mountain of pillows. Keona turned on a cartoon EJ liked and sat back, relaxing with him in her arms. She usually cleared the bed of so many pillows and blankets when EJ slept with them to reduce his risk of getting tangled or smothered; she would make sure to do it before she felt herself falling asleep.

"Dada?" EJ asked in his little voice, sounding sad. Keona sighed.

"I miss him too, baby boy," she whispered, kissing the top of his head. "I miss him too."

Keona was awakened by soft lips on hers. She smiled, then opened her eyes. A split second later she sat up, gasping. "EJ—"

Elliott brought her into his arms, calming her.

"In his own bed, Key. He was safe; you had him on top of you. I moved him so you could lie down fully."

"Oh," Keona said, putting her hand over her pounding heart. "Thank you, love."

"You must have been tired. You usually clean off the bed when you bring him in here," Elliott observed. Keona threw her arms around him, breathing him in. She was so damn glad he was home.

"I thought I'd have a chance before I drifted off. I'm not usually so careless. I—"

"Key, it's okay. I have no doubt you would have woken up at some point and done it. It wasn't a criticism, it was more of a worry. You and Baby Boy have a long day or a rough night?"

"We had both, if by 'rough night,' you mean he spent it whining, 'I want Dada,' and refusing to go to sleep," Keona said. Elliott chuckled.

"Missed me, huh?" he said. Keona pulled back so she could look into his face. His juicy lips were tilted upward in an arrogant smirk.

"Yes, he did," she confirmed. Elliott kissed her forehead.

"He the only one?"

"You know better," Keona said. Elliott leaned down and pressed his mouth to hers, stealing her breath with a sweet and sensual kiss. Keona moaned and opened her lips, letting his tongue inside. She sighed and pressed against him, her nose filling with the scent of his body wash and matching lotion, letting her know he'd been home long enough to shower before getting into bed with her.

"No more leaving before he's down for the night. He misses you too much," Keona said against Elliott's mouth.

Elliott chuckled. "I will make sure I don't leave before he closes his eyes," he promised. He went back to kissing her, and soon Keona was on her back, taking Elliott's deep strokes and calling his name while he drank from her breasts. Every time they made love was better than the last. Every touch and kiss was a reminder of the power of their love, a reminder of home. *Their* home. Keona was so damn glad she made her way back to their home.

"Come sit on my face, Key," Elliott ordered her, pulling out and lying down. Keona sat up, crawling up and wrapping her thighs around his head, her face toward his feet. Elliott's tongue snaked out, slurping her cream, and she jerked, whimpering. He smacked her ass and held her thighs still, pushing his tongue inside her and pulling out to swirl it around her clit. Keona bit her lip, then leaned forward to take the head of Elliott's dick into her mouth. She tasted herself and sucked more of him, suctioning her mouth perfectly. Elliott groaned and licked her clit, his fingers digging into her thighs. They got into a rhythm, and it was as effortless as always. She moaned around a mouthful of dick, desperate to come. He sucked her pussy lips into his mouth while his tongue swiped over her bud again and again. The way this man knew exactly how to please made her want to show out for him. Only for him.

Keona rocked her hips, grinding onto his face as she tried to keep her sucking rhythm. Elliott smacked her ass hard and sent his tongue inside of her. It was a rush of ecstasy, mind-numbing and perfect. She came, moaning, her lower half shaking. She didn't want him to ever stop making love to her with his mouth. She wanted to be his Lollipop forever. Keona heard the smacks and slurps as he savored her juices, and she sucked her man harder, making him grip her thighs and moan her name.

"Lollipop... you gon get a mouthful if you keep on," he warned. Keona kept going, tasting his hot, smooth skin and loving the way he stretched her mouth. She sucked him greedily, taking him into her throat, making him moan. Elliott slid two fingers into her soaked pussy, pressed against her walls, and caressed her. Keona hummed with pleasure, determined to take every drop of her man. She continued making him groan and twitch, licking and savoring him like *he* was the lollipop while she bounced her hips, riding his thick fingers.

"Come for me, Elliott," she whispered, freeing her mouth for a second and then going back to sucking on his dick. Elliott thrust up into her throat, finger fucking her faster.

"Ahhh, fuck. Key, gotdamn—"

"Mmmm," she responded as best she could with her mouth full. She sucked faster, harder, knowing he was close. The second she came up for air, Elliott freed his hand from her pussy and moved her away, pushing her thick body to the side. Keona squealed, ending up on her back with him climbing over her. He spread and lifted her thighs then slid inside her pussy firmly, staring into her eyes the entire time. She loved it when he was focused like this, when she was the absolute center of his attention.

"No swallowing," he whispered. "I want all my babies in your womb. I want all of me inside you." He started fucking her hard, taking them both back to the edge in a few thrusts. Keona grabbed for him, a cry building in her throat, the edges of her vision blurring. The sounds of their sex filled the room, and she could hear Elliott mumbling her name under his breath over and over. She was spinning higher, falling deeper, and her man was all she could see and feel.

"Ohhhhh! Elliott! Yes, yes," she yelled out, her orgasm slamming into her, shaking her entire body. In the distance, she heard Elliott grunt and then felt his warm cum spurting into her pussy. He leaned down, taking her nipples into his mouth one by one and drinking her milk. The pull and swipe of his tongue made her come harder, her pussy clenching his dick tightly as she screamed again. Elliott moaned and pulled out, falling to the side of her, trying to catch his breath.

"I got you, Lollipop. I got you," he soothed, gathering her in his arms. Keona turned into his chest, her body still quivering with aftershocks. The two of them lay together quietly, getting their bearings.

A short while later, after Elliott coaxed her into the shower and washed her thoroughly, they snuggled against their mountain of pillows, holding each other. Keona was being lulled to sleep by Elliott's warmth, his whispers of love in her ear, and the soft sounds of the TV as he watched sports highlights. She sighed, her eyes drifting closed. She was home, and her man was home too. The ground was solid and steady. Life was good.

Epilogue

<u>**Keona**</u>
<u>**Seven Months Later**</u>

"Please sit down. Why won't the two of you rest? There are other adults at this party, you know," Kimberly Ross said as she grabbed the hands of her very pregnant daughter and her equally pregnant friend. Keona and Nasima giggled as they waddled behind her, finally allowing themselves to be led to a table with two chairs. They sat down, and someone brought them plates piled with wings, scalloped potatoes, and fried corn. The kids were eating chicken nuggets, pizza, mini mac and cheese cups, and fruit, but Keona wanted something more substantial for the adults in attendance. The two friends dug in, relaxing after making sure the party was everything they planned.

It was EJ's second birthday, and there were dinosaurs everywhere, along with a ten-car ride-on train set traveling around the entire party. EJ was among his daycare friends and the children of some of the men who worked for the organization, his father close by. Trevino and Bashir helped Elliott with the children, taking breaks to look up and find Nasima with their eyes. They doted on her and refused to let her out of their sight since she was nearly due to have their baby.

"Now eat. Everything is perfect, and we got it. Where's the other pregnant one? I saw her with her girlfriend not long ago. She's not as far along, but she needs to sit down too," Kimberly continued fussing. Keona grinned.

"I don't see Romelo either, so my guess is he grabbed them both and took them somewhere to feel them up," she said.

Kimberly shook her head. "That's why all of you are like this now. Let me go make sure she has something to eat too," she said before hurrying off. Keona and Nasima giggled again and dug into their food.

"I'm glad your mom is here," Nasima said. Keona nodded, thinking of how far they'd come as a family. She knew Nasima understood the void. She'd been born to two addicts who died before they could fully recover into the parents she needed. Nas was determined their children would know different, and she held everyone in their circle to a high standard.

"I am too," Keona replied. The two friends went back to eating, content to rest and watch the party they'd planned.

After her nighttime visit, Kimberly stayed away for a month. Romelo gave her the things the Wolf had in her name, and she seemed to have disappeared. Keona was sad, but not surprised. She'd had little faith her mother would surface again, but she did, saying she decided to settle in town and be closer to them. She told Keona she had found a therapist and asked her to come to the sessions too when she was ready. Keona refused at first, but her own therapy journey made her change her mind.

Months later, she and Kimberly had a basic friendly relationship. Keona wouldn't say she felt they were true mother and daughter—there was much more work to be done—but she'd been honest and supportive thus far, she was making amends for her past behaviors, she clearly loved her grandson, and she was here today, making sure Keona's vision came true. It was more than she could have hoped for.

"You good, Lollipop?" Her man's voice rumbled into her ear and Keona smiled as she chewed, feeling her body heat up.

"Yes, baby, I'm fine. Are you okay?"

"When you, our baby boy, and our new little one are okay, I'm good. It's all I need," Elliott said back, taking a chair beside her.

Keona giggled and leaned into him, still eating. Neither of them knew the sex of their baby and weren't too concerned. Pregnancy and labor were too much of a challenge to give energy to thoughts of who the baby would or wouldn't be. Their only concerns were whether they would be alive and healthy.

"You've been running around behind these kids all afternoon. Did you get something to eat, at least?"

"Key, I'm good. I snacked on a few things and MomMom made me a plate. She made you one too, for later."

"Oh, that's a good idea. Vino! Bash!" Nas heard the tail end of their conversation and called for her men. They appeared moments later, looking scared.

"What's wrong, Lil Baby? What happened?" Trevino said, squatting beside her and running his hands over her body. Nasima swallowed a mouthful of potatoes and chicken.

"Nothing. Can one of you make me a plate to take home?" she asked sweetly.

Trevino and Bashir stared at their girlfriend and then rolled their eyes. Trevino walked off, shaking his head, and everyone laughed after him. Bashir smirked.

"Nas, why you call us like it was an emergency?" he asked.

Nasima shrugged. "It was. Can you make it?"

Bashir leaned down and kissed her forehead softly, then her lips. "My pretty little greedy fat mama can have whatever she wants." He smiled and kissed her again before walking away. Keona and Elliott burst into more laughter, and Nasima went back to eating as if nothing happened.

"Good thing I'm not that spoiled," Keona said innocently. Elliott snorted in disbelief.

"*You're* saying this? The same person who threw a whole tantrum and almost cried because she thought there were no Swedish fish on the candy table. Are we talking about her?"

"Elliott, why you bringing up old shit?" Keona said, pouting. Elliott laughed and kissed her cheek, wrapping his arm around her. She turned and pressed her lips to his, the heat rising in her body and in the room. This man made her hotter than ever. His hand moved to the side of her breast, squeezing softly. Keona giggled against his mouth. She'd finally weaned EJ months ago, so she didn't have milk and wouldn't have any until the new baby came, but it didn't matter. Elliott still loved her breasts, and she was certain she'd never wean *him*. He was almost as excited for the milk as he was for the baby.

Boy, stop groping her out in the open!" MomMom chastised as she walked up to the two of them. Elliott pulled back from their kiss and dropped his hand. Keona and Nasima laughed.

"Yes, ma'am," he replied to his grandmother, and she gave him the side eye as she went past the table. EJ ran up to them next. Keona leaned down for a kiss, and he stood on his toes, meeting her halfway.

"Daddy, come play!" he said, his voice loud and clear. Elliott stood up, smirking.

"A'ight, baby boy. I'm coming," he said, kissing Keona one last time before being dragged away. She looked after her two boys, her heart bursting with love.

This was home. Her solid ground. And she was here to stay.

The End

Sneak Peek- His Fire & His Ice

The Finale of the Elements Series

His Fire and His Ice

Romelo Davis is a kingpin, a boss, a man other men fear. He can have whatever he wants whenever he wants it. He's never shared anything in his life except his girlfriend. Bianca loved him without a doubt, but she loved Sadie too, and there was no getting around it. He and Sadie were content with their open arrangement, getting along with each other for the sake of their woman. Then one day, she was gone. Burned by her abandonment and betrayal, he and Sadie healed their hearts by melding them together. And they're happy. But now Bianca's back. Will everything change?

Sadie Wells never loved anything more than guns, and freedom. Then she met Bianca Bellamy. Lost in love, she thought the two of them could conquer anything, and with Romelo on the other side to balance things out, life was perfect. Then, Bianca left, and she and Romelo were alone. They fused their hearts together, building something new over the remains of Bianca's abandonment. But now she's back. And Sadie doesn't know if she's coming to take her away from Romelo... or take Romelo away from her.

Bianca Bellamy had two lovers who made her heart light and her life perfect. But her dreams of dancing would not be denied, so she left them, running away to chase her destiny. A year later, she misses them both too much to stay away and heads home. But everything's different now. Can she get her loves back and open her heart to new possibilities?

Prologue
One Year Ago
<u>*Romelo*</u>

"Romelo! Is she here?! Are you hiding her?" Sadie Marie Wells screamed as she walked through the house and into Romelo "King" Davis's office. Her steps were hard, and her face flushed with anger and hurt. Romelo could see her coming down the hall toward him, her big titties heaving with exertion, braids swinging, wide hips switching, her plushness bouncing all over as she waved a piece of paper in her hand. Her cute little upturned rose was red against her light brown skin, and he could tell she'd been crying. Still, his girlfriend's girlfriend was gorgeous. If Bianca had anything, it was impeccable taste in women. Scratch and Teddy, Romelo's guards, followed behind her, rolling their eyes at her tirade. He'd told them to expect her.

"Sadie, come sit down. Why don't you—"

"No. NO. I want to know if she's here. Is she under that damn desk sucking your dick, afraid to face me? Is that why you're so calm, Romelo?"

"Of course not. Sadie—"

"Get your ass out here, Bianca Bellamy! What, did she pick you and not want to tell me? Did you convince her she didn't need me? BIANCA!!!"

"Gotdammit, Sadie, stop yelling. If you let me speak—" he started, his ears ringing from her screaming, but Sadie slapped the letter down on the desk, turning to look out into the hallway where even Scratch and Teddy were now cowering in the face of her anger.

"Fuck that! You'd better tell her to come out here and break up with me like a grown fucking woman. I deserve better. If she—"

"Sadie!" Romelo barked, finally interrupting her. He sighed deeply and slid an identical letter onto the desk, looking right into her red-rimmed eyes. "She's not here. She left me too."

Sadie swallowed, her words running out as she stared at him. She sank into a chair in front of his desk, and he went around to her, sitting in the one beside her and taking her hand.

"She's gone? She...you too?" she whispered, her breaths speeding up. Sadie closed her eyes, letting two tears fall. Her hands shook and her body slumped, as if her anger had tired her.

"I got in from a meeting a couple of hours ago. The letter was waiting for me when I got back. I haven't seen her since she left to spend the night with you yesterday. She must have come in sometime today and left it." Romelo spoke softly, rubbing Sadie's palm with his thumb. Knowing their girlfriend really was gone, she was visibly distressed and seemed lost. He couldn't deny he wasn't feeling much better.

Romelo met Bianca Bellamy two years before, and he fell in love immediately. His heart connecting fast was a family trait; his cousin Trevino had known his man Bashir would take his heart the day he met him. So, Romelo had no qualms about laying his heart bare to Bianca. He just worried she wouldn't return the favor. After all, she was a dancer who wanted her name in lights, and he was a drug kingpin and weapons trafficker. But Bianca fell in love with him too. She told him she was polyamorous, and he was fine in an open relationship. His side was closed; he'd wanted only her, but he wasn't a jealous or selfish man. Romelo knew what he brought to the table. There were whispers about him losing respect among his team for "letting his woman play him with that sharing shit," but the King caught the whisperers and responded out loud with fury and gasoline, watching calmly as they danced to death in the flames. There were no more whispers after that.

Six months into their relationship, Bianca introduced him to Sadie Wells—a vibrant, hot-tempered, stubborn, spoiled she-devil who loved guns and wouldn't hesitate to use one. The fire to Bianca's ice. She assured him he and Sadie were all she wanted in the world, and it was all the motivation *they* needed to make their three-way relationship as harmonious as possible. They'd become friends, collaborating on gifts and celebrations for their number one girl. Romelo thought they were all happy. But now Bianca was gone, like a thief in the night, leaving nothing but two letters to explain why she'd broken two hearts.

I guess we weren't all happy.

"I don't understand why she would do this," Sadie said, her voice a tearful mumble. Romelo kept rubbing her palm, hoping to soothe her and himself.

"My guess is she wanted a clean break," he replied. "With her auditioning for the lead with this new dance troupe, she probably thought she'd be on the road so much our relationships would suffer. So, she ended them now to save us all some heartbreak later."

Sadie sucked her teeth. "She ended them because she's a damn scaredy cat. Yes, things would have changed, been more challenging, but I knew what Bibi did when I met her. I wasn't going anywhere."

"Neither was I. But it doesn't matter what we knew. It matters what she believed. And she believed she was doing the right thing."

"How the fuck are you so calm about this?" Sadie demanded. Romelo chuckled, rolling his shoulders to release the tension.

"There's some shot-up targets in my gun range out back that would suggest I'm not calm at all," he answered. Sadie giggled, pulling her hands from his to wipe her face.

"Can we go out there? I need to shoot something too."

Romelo stood up, reaching for Sadie's hand again. He pulled her from the chair and into his arms quickly, kissing the top of her head. They'd had their hearts broken by the same woman. As strange a bond as it was, they were bonded. He'd take care of Sadie. Romelo had a feeling it was what Bianca would want.

"Of course. Let's go," he said, and he and Sadie headed to the shooting range behind his house.

Three Months Later

Sadie

"Romelo! I brought lunch!" Sadie yelled as she headed to his office. Scratch and Teddy shook their heads; they were used to her loudness by now. She opened the office door and went in, setting the bag with their lunch on the desk and sitting down. Romelo was talking on one cell phone while he texted on another, a hollowed-out book filled with small bags of white powder and stacks of money open in front of him. He smiled at her, and his brown eyes lit up.

Romelo "King" Davis was easily the finest man she'd ever seen in her life. His skin was the color of sandstone, brown and orange hues mixing deliciously in a perfect swirl, setting off his chubby cheeks and toffee eyes. He had a wide nose, slightly crooked from a teenage break that didn't heal correctly, and thick, curved lips that were positively sinful. Romelo was huge—six foot two and wide-bodied, bulked by muscles and fat in equal measure. His chest was hard, but his belly was soft, and she loved sinking into him whenever he hugged her.

"You got 'til Tuesday. And because you feel like you can play with me, Truck will be there to collect. Yeah, yeah, whatever." Romelo put both phones down and closed the hollowed-out book. With Sadie there every day, he no longer worried about what she saw—he knew she'd keep it to herself. Sadie started unpacking food after he wiped the desktop and his hands. He dug into the steak sandwich she brought him, taking two huge bites and grunting as he ate.

She watched him eat, suddenly noticing the thickness of his lips as he wrapped them around the sandwich, the sharpness of his white teeth sinking into the bread, steak, cheese, and onions, his strong jaw moving as he chewed, his toffee eyes closing in relief as he eased his hunger. Sadie noticed everything today, and it was like she'd never seen any of it before. Today, it was different. Today, it was...affecting her.

"What's the point of you having someone here to cook if you skip meals?" Sadie questioned, trying to regulate her thoughts as she took a much more delicate bite of her own sandwich. Romelo swallowed his food and rolled his eyes.

"Woman, what I tell you about lecturing me when I'm eating?"

"Somebody has to. You need to take better care of yourself. You're working to keep yourself distracted and busy and you're wasting away. I don't like it."

"Your grumpy ass doesn't like anything," he mumbled, taking another bite. Sadie opened her mouth to deny, then shut it when she realized she couldn't. Romelo was exhausted and mired in work, and she was crabby and ill-tempered, irritated by everything—especially happy things.

In the three months Bianca had been gone, she and Romelo had grown closer, leaning on each other as friends and confidants, their connection cemented over late-night drinking sessions, movie nights in his theater room, and hours spent out back, shooting targets to vent their anger.

At first, Sadie begged him to track Bibi down. She knew with Romelo's considerable resources, it was very possible for him to find out where she'd gone. But he denied her, saying if Bianca wanted space, they should give it to her, and that they both deserved better than having to chase after her. Sadie didn't want to agree but had to concede he was right. Bianca had to learn the hard way no one would love her better than them, and Sadie knew the lesson was coming. But in the meantime, Romelo pushed deeper into work, and she snapped at everyone...for everything.

"I'm going out back after we finish," she announced. "I want to shoot something."

"Not today," Romelo refused, swallowing his last bite. "I can't take the noise. My head is killing me."

Sadie pouted; Romelo never denied her anything. But she didn't protest. It was his house, after all. And if his head was hurting, his rest was more important since his migraines had joined his eating and sleeping habits as another thing that was getting worse.

They sat in the office for a few more minutes, then Romelo took a bottle of water from the mini fridge beside him and said he was going up to his room. She had free rein in his house, and everything was alarmed and guarded, so he had no issue leaving her alone. He knew she was safe. Sadie thought about going home, but she didn't want to be alone. She decided she would hole up in Romelo's theater room and watch movies and implement her usual plan of bugging Scratch and Teddy until one of them watched with her.

Halfway into the movie, Sadie decided to check on Romelo. She hopped up, heading to the second level and knocking on the French doors that opened to his primary suite. There was no answer, and Sadie tried the door, finding it unlocked. She ducked in, shutting the door behind her, and walked quietly through his sitting room into the bedroom area. Romelo was in bed, the room dark and quiet to help relieve the pain in his head. She could see his eyes were closed, but his breathing was so stuttered and choppy she knew he wasn't sleeping.

"Melo?" Sadie called to him softly. Romelo opened his eyes, staring at her. He sat up and lifted his hand, gesturing to her. As if he'd given her feet permission to move, Sadie hurried to the side of the bed, kicking off her sneakers and climbing in. He immediately pulled her on top of him, holding her so tight she could barely breathe.

"Is this okay?" he whispered.

Sadie nodded into his chest. It was better than okay. His body was warm and hard against her softness. It'd been so long since someone held her, relief and pure instinct made her snuggle closer. Romelo growled deep in his throat, pleased with her touch. Sadie breathed in his scent, closing her own eyes. The two of them were closer these days, and very affectionate, but this felt different. It felt like sweetness and desire, like warm honey and slow kisses. It felt like something that wasn't about Bianca at all.

"Is your head better?" she asked, keeping her voice soft. Romelo rubbed slow circles on her back, the pressure of his hands more comforting than a weighted blanket.

"Nah, not really," he answered her. Sadie sat up, looking into his eyes. She saw the same unsure desire she was feeling, along with pain from his headache. She lifted her hands to either side of his head, using her fingers to massage his temples. He sighed, gripping her hips as she straddled him. His eyes drifted closed and his face relaxed. Sadie smiled. Next time, she'd bring some lavender oil to soothe him even more. She continued her massage, humming in a soft voice while Romelo rubbed her hips and thighs. Sadie felt her desire increasing, making her want to grind on his lap and create more friction against his dick, which was slowly hardening underneath her. But she forced herself to focus. Romelo was hurting, and he needed her.

"Your hands feel so good, Shug," Romelo whispered into the quiet. Sadie blinked, momentarily confused. He'd never called her anything but her name before. Her body warmed with affection at the thought of getting her own nickname. He'd always called

Bianca "Baby Girl." She pushed away thoughts of their ex and re-focused on making Romelo feel better. He was squeezing her ass now, lifting his hips so she could feel that he was fully hard.

Sadie gulped. She and Romelo were friends. They leaned on each other, took care of each other. They were healing together. Desiring more seemed greedy, given how their closeness started. But she wanted Romelo, and it seemed he wanted her too. Neither of them had any idea what was happening, but there was no way Sadie would be the one to stop it. She leaned forward, kissing him before she could talk herself out of it. He only hesitated a second before kissing her back, his lips firm and warm on hers. They moaned at the same time.

Lips pressed and tasted, and soon their tongues were in the game. Sadie's hands fell from Romelo's head to his shoulders, and she gripped him tightly, pleasure blooming from the crown of her head to the soles of her feet. Kissing Romelo felt like something she'd been waiting her entire life to do. Their mouths made love and Sadie whimpered, eager for more. Romelo's tongue was thick and wrapped around hers, pulling them both deeper into the swarm of their desire. His hands were busy, caressing her curves, gripping her body, palming her softness.

Sadie was burning up now, and she wanted his skin against hers. She sat back, pulling her top over her head. Her pink lace bra was a simple scrap, barely holding her large breasts, and Romelo smiled as he stared at her hard nipples. He reached up and grabbed the bra in the middle, ripping it open. Sadie gasped in surprise and then pleasure as his mouth covered her breast. He suckled her, hard, and she moaned. She arched her back, pushing her breast further into his hot mouth. Romelo's fingers pulled at her other nipple, prepping it for its turn between his lips.

"Dammit, Melo," Sadie protested weakly, "that fucking bra costs me fifty bucks."

"Then it's a good thing I ripped that cheap shit," he replied, his mouth still against her. He licked her between his words, making her dig her nails into his shoulders. "You getting in this bed means you mine now, and when you mine, everything touching your body should reflect that you got a nigga with *infinite* pockets. You hearing me, Sadie Marie?"

His arrogant edict, the growl of her full name, and his tongue on her nipple sent Sadie into orbit, and she nodded, too aroused to form words. Romelo pulled back, staring into her eyes. His were dark and stormy, filled with desire and something else she wouldn't dare name out loud.

"No nodding. I need to know you with me. Do you understand, Shug?" he whispered, reverting to her new nickname, and Sadie swallowed. He tugged on her nipples as he spoke and she wet her panties, her breathing harsh and choppy. She heard the urgency in his voice, the desperation...the anxiety. He needed to know he wasn't in this alone.

"I understand," she whispered back.

"Understand what?" he demanded. Sadie licked her lips, moved in his lap, felt his hard dick. She couldn't wait to have it inside of her.

"That I'm yours, and everything touching me should reflect that."

"Good girl," Romelo praised her and went back to sucking and licking on her. Sadie moaned his name, her senses overloaded with pleasure and new love. She understood Romelo was offering his heart and body and she wanted both with a fierceness she'd never expected. He pushed her to the side and underneath him, flipping their positions so that he was on top. His mouth released her breast, Sadie's whimper of protest swallowed when he kissed her again. Their lips and tongues tangled, and her hands went around

Romelo's neck, running her fingers over his nape, eliciting groans from him.

"Shug, I need you bad. Can I have you?" Romelo whispered against her lips. Sadie nipped at his mouth, licked his sexy smile.

"Of course, you can, baby. I'm yours, remember?" she whispered back. Romelo grinned, leaning up to tug off her pants and underwear. Seconds later, her big thighs were spread wide, and he was buried deep, catching them both off guard with how good it felt. Sadie came almost immediately, her body on edge, her senses dancing. Romelo sank into her wet pussy like it was home, and as far as either of them were concerned, now it was.

Sadie held him to her, moaning at his deep thrusts. She heard what he hadn't said. The invitation to his bed was his declaration that he was hers to have. Hers to keep. Hers to love. He'd just needed to know she felt the same. And she did. Romelo Davis had healed her heart. It was only right that it become his now.

And nine months later... Bianca is the next to come home. But is there still room for her?

The Air Between Us Bonus Scenes

Hi! The following bonus scenes were cut from the final edit of The Air Between Us. They all take place at different points of the story. The release of these scenes is a huge thank you for all the love you guys have shown Nas, Vino, and Bash. I hope you enjoy!

The Air Between Us- Closer To My Dream

Bashir "You were dreaming about her again, weren't you?" Bashir asked, coming up behind Trevino and rubbing his shoulders. His lover was sitting at the kitchen island, his muscles bunched tight with agitation. Bashir knew Trevino was exhausted from a night of work but restless from his mind refusing to let him sleep. Trevino leaned into his touch, sighing.

"I can't get her to stop running," he said, his voice strained with weariness. "Butta, she won't stop running away from me. You think it means something?"

"Trev, why don't we go get her? Or at least go see her? Maybe once you know she's alright—"

"If I see her again, I'm not letting go. I refuse to let go this time. It's why I stay away. Because I don't want to interrupt her life. If I see her again, she's coming with me. I won't be able to walk away."

"She may not want you to. Who knows? Nasima may miss you as much as you miss her—"

"Then why does she keep running away from me? Why won't she come to me?"

"Trev, it was a dream, baby," Bashir said, hugging him around his back and pressing soft kisses into his spine. "And it being a dream means her turning away has more to do with your own subconscious than with Nasima herself."

"How so?" Trevino asked.

Bashir moved away and went to the refrigerator, getting them both a beer. Then he sat next to his man, leaning in so their knees were touching. Touch was very important to Trevino.

"Nasima turning away and not coming to you could be the manifestation of the guilt you feel about sending her away, or about not keeping up with her. Maybe you're afraid she needs you, or needed you before, and you weren't there."

"I didn't keep up with her because I never wanted her to know I was clinging to her and not the other way around. Butta, I needed her more than she ever needed me. Nas is strong and so smart; she can do anything. I was the one who needed her to live, to feel balanced...to feel normal. I never wanted her to know—"

"You depended on her, on her love," Bashir finished. He nodded and sighed. Trevino loved so deeply it was impossible not to feel it. And Bashir never took being one of the few people who got to experience it for granted. These dreams of Nasima had been plaguing him for months. They'd increased in the last couple of weeks; it was nearly every night now. Bashir believed it meant she was close. Or about to be.

Trevino took a long gulp of his beer. "Does it bother you to know how much I love her?"

"It would if I didn't know how much you love me," Bashir said honestly. Trevino nodded again. The two of them finished their beers and went back upstairs, tugging off each other's underwear and getting into bed.

In their gigantic bed, they huddled together in the middle, kissing and touching each other. Bashir opened his mouth for Trevino's tongue, moaning softly. Their kisses were wet and urgent, their emotional talk making way for heightened passion. He moved his hands over his man's chest, thumbing his nipples, massaging his stomach. Trev was hard everywhere, and it made Bashir's desire rise. His own body was bulkier since he'd stopped boxing, softer around the arms, thighs, and belly, and the juxtaposition made for perfect lovemaking. Bashir spit a little into his palm, and grabbed Trevino's dick, pumping gently as they kissed.

"More," Trev demanded, pressing closer. Bashir did as he was told, caressing his man, rubbing his thumb over the sensitive tip, spreading the precum already there, opening his fist more as Trevino hardened fully in his capable hands. He heard Trev moan right before his hips thrust forward, eager for more touches. Bashir jerked harder, sucking and pulling at Trevino's lips with his own. His own dick was leaking at this point, so he moved his body forward rubbing his dick against Trevino's. They both groaned, their kisses turning frantic and sloppy. Trevino lifted Bashir's thigh over his, grinding against him, the friction of their dicks touching enhancing the pleasurable sensations.

"Trev," Bashir called out, nearly overcome. There was nothing better than making love with Trevino.

"I'm right here, Butta. And I ain't going nowhere. You're my life, you hear me? My life," Trevino answered him, kissing his jaw and the corner of his mouth, grinding against him harder. Bashir was close to coming, his balls tightening with anticipation, pleasure filling him as his dick rubbed against another. A last frenzied kiss and they both ejaculated, their thick cum spurting on their stomachs and thighs.

"Baby, I love you," Bashir moaned, feeling his ears clog and his hands shake. He came so hard his vision blurred, and Trevino didn't let him go the entire time.

"I love you too. I love you too," he answered. They fell apart, breathing heavily. A few minutes later, the two of them were kissing and whispering their love in the shower together, washing the evidence of their passion away. Soon after, they were on clean sheets, snuggled together, dark curtains keeping out the light of the new day until they were ready for it.

"Trev," Bashir asked, yawning, "do you think Nasima could be the one? You know, the missing piece we talked about?"

"I don't know, Butta. But I know if I see her again, I'm going to ask her."

"And I know if you dream about her one more time, we're going to get her so I can ask her myself."

The Air Between Us- Date Night

Nasima

"But I don't understand. We're all together. Why don't we *all* have Date Night?" Nasima questioned.

She was in the garage, sitting on a wooden worktable, her short, thick legs swinging as she watched her two men work on a car. They were dirty and sweaty, tightening and loosening things, passing each other tools, speaking car language in low grunts, heads buried deep in the bowels of the engine. It was glorious. She loved watching them, experiencing their unique rhythm, feeling the undeniable lust and love covering everything they did. And their telepathic need to look up at the same time and make sure she was okay only heightened the attractiveness of their manly man bodies doing man things. Nasima sighed, getting the urge to rub her sensitive nipples. She tried to stop being so horny around them, but it was hard.

"Lil Baby, we all need the opportunity to develop our relationships with each other. The three of us are a no-brainer. Me and Butta got sparring and the cars. You and I have the bonds of our past. You and Butta need something of your own. And until y'all figure out what it's gon be, I'm mandating a Date Night strictly for the two of you," Trevino said, dropping a wrench back in the toolbox and picking up another. Bashir said nothing, but Nasima could see his smirk from where she was sitting.

"You think I'm going to be like the man you had here before, jealous because you and Bash have things without me. I'm not him."

"I know, Lil Baby, but—"

"He wasn't right for you two, but I am. I can handle y'all having things. It's not like you don't let me watch," Nasima said with a grin. Bashir chuckled but didn't respond. Trevino rolled his eyes.

"Woman, this is not about the past, although you have a point. He wasn't right for us, and I know you're not him. You and Butta need time alone, and I'm making sure you get it."

"But what will you do?"

"Miss us," Bashir finally added to the conversation. He winked at her, and Nasima was warm all over.

"Hell yeah, I will. But that's beside the point. Y'all need this. You deserve it."

"But Bash and I have our private time when you work overnight," Nasima insisted. Trevino shook his head.

"The two of you comforting each other because you're missing *me* is not the same as y'all creating your own bond. Don't argue, Lil Baby. I said what I said."

"What *you* said was I belong to both of you. I'm yours—you and Bash. And now you're making up reasons to put space between us. Do you need time to yourself? Is it you who needs to be alone? You can tell me," Nasima said. Bashir laughed. He was determined to stay out of this, which was only frustrating Nasima. It wasn't like she didn't love being with Bash. She was simply having a hard time processing Vino wanting to be away from her when they'd only just found each other again.

"Lil Baby, I would live inside your skin and wear Butta as a coat if I could do it—I don't need alone time, love. I promise. I want you and Bashir to be as solid as you can be, so I know you'll stay together and take care of each other even if I'm not around," Trevino explained. Nasima stared at him, fear coming over her. Was she losing him already? What was he so afraid of? Bashir stood up straight, a frown coming over his light brown face.

"Trev? What the fuck? You going somewhere?" he demanded.

"Now you want to help," Nasima said, rolling her eyes at Bashir.

"I stayed out of it before because I thought he was being dramatic and you were being spoiled. But this is different. Trev, what's different? Did something happen?" Bashir asked as he wiped his face and hands on a towel and went around the car to his lover. Trevino sighed.

"Nothing happened, Butta. I swear, we're okay. And we're going to stay okay for a long time. I need to make sure you two always have each other to lean on. And I want your foundation to last, which means it needs to be based on something other than me."

"It already is. I love Bash, and he loves me. He takes away my fear and loneliness."

"She takes away my angst and nervousness. Loving her makes me calm," Bashir said.

"Loving him keeps me grounded. What we have is because of you, yes, but it's very real and very much about us. You don't need to worry," Nasima soothed him. Trevino sighed again.

"I'll never give Nas up, and I'll never leave her alone. You have my word on that, Trev. And you have my word it'll be because I want to. Because I can't live without her either," Bashir said, looking over at her. Nasima smiled and blew him a kiss. This man made her melt.

Trevino pulled Bashir close, kissing him quickly. And now her panties were wet.

"Maybe we've done enough work on the car today," Trevino said, his voice getting lower and more suggestive. Bashir grinned.

"Lil Baby, we're gonna shower down here so we don't track dirt through the house. You need to be upstairs waiting for us," he ordered gently, never looking away from Trevino. Nasima used a stool to get herself off the table and onto the floor. She started into the house, thinking of the lingerie she'd wear to drive them wild when they got to the bedroom.

"And since it's our Date Night, Bash can have me first," she said as she entered the house, and her two men laughed behind her.

The Air Between Us- Movie Night

Trevino

"Bash—oh, please fuck me!"

Trevino opened his eyes, registering being barely awake. He sprawled out at one end of their massive sectional and Bashir and Nasima were at the other, making love.

He remembered coming in from work and joining Movie Night with his lovers. Then when he was drifting off, he got a blanket and moved to the other end of the couch, not wanting his snoring to disturb them. They'd both urged him to go get in bed, but he didn't want to be in it without them. Now, the movie was watching Bashir and Nasima as they fucked, their sounds of pleasure dotting the air between the noises of whatever film they'd chosen.

"You're gonna wake him, mama. If you can't control it, I'll have to stop," Bashir warned playfully, sliding in deep. Nasima's breath hitched as she whimpered.

"If you stop, I'll kill you," she swore. Bashir laughed and picked up his speed, leaning down to kiss her lips. His back muscles rippled as he moved inside their girl, filling her sweet little pussy until she was out of breath. Trevino stayed still, content to watch their passion, content to wrap himself in the sight and sound of their love. He didn't know if deriving almost as much pleasure from watching them as he did from having them made him some kind of creep, but he didn't care. They were beautiful together. Wet, loud, nasty, and free with each other. Bashir fucked their Lil Baby like his life depended on pleasing her, and Nas's pussy was pure nirvana, taking everything he had to give and giving paradise in return. Watching them was magic.

Nasima moaned, grabbed for Butta's beard. His stroke was unraveling her fast, and her wet pussy made all the greedy, gushy sounds they both loved. She was desperate for it, and her orgasm was close.

"Bash, please—I need— Oh, baby, it's happening," she babbled, shaking her head back and forth. Bashir moaned, fucked her faster, spread her thighs wider.

"I want it all over me, Lil Baby. Give it to me, Nas," he ordered, his words strained as her pussy wrapped around him again and again. Trevino let out a quiet moan of his own, loving the moment before the climax, the moment they knew the pleasure was about to drown them, the moment before the ecstasy. Nasima looked over at him, probably to remind herself not to scream, and her eyes found his open ones. He grinned at her, licking his lips.

"I want to hear it too," he said aloud. Bashir turned, saw him, and pounded into Nasima's pussy, never taking his eyes off him. Trevino nodded his head, and Nas screamed, her orgasmic cry drowning out whomever was running for their life on the TV screen. Butta kept going, leaning back to rub her clit and make her come apart completely. He growled, his mouth stretching into a grin, and Trevino knew she'd soaked his thighs and probably the couch with her release.

"Since you're awake...wanna taste her?" Butta said to him, and Trevino nodded, sitting up and moving swiftly to their side of the sectional. Nasima was still whimpering incoherently, trying to catch her breath. Bashir pulled out and backed up, expecting him to take his place between Nasima's thighs. Instead, Trevino yanked Bashir over in front of him.

"You first," he said and swallowed Butta's dick. He was slick with Nasima's cream and her juices and Trevino slurped it up greedily, taking his man to the back of his throat.

"Trev—fuck, babe. I can't—I'm there," Bashir stuttered, already on the brink from fucking Nasima. He was primed to explode, and Trevino wanted every drop. He sucked harder, rubbed his balls, slid his tongue along the veins. His Butta tasted so good, especially when he was covered in their girl. Reaching over with one hand, he found the drenched center of Nasima's thighs and swiped his thumb over her swollen clit. She wailed, trying to close her legs and move away from the sensations. Butta watched him play with her, his dick trapped in a warm and wet mouth, and then came with a roar, shooting his cum down Trevino's throat and thrusting his hips forward. His body jerked and his hands went to Trevino's head, rubbing his deep waves.

"Oh, my fucking— *Trev*," he begged as Trevino sucked the soul out of him. He loved it when Butta lost it like this, when he let go completely. He swallowed every drop of him and then pulled back, licking his lips, his fingers still lightly stroking Nas. Bashir dragged in deep breaths and moved to the side, falling onto the chair.

Trevino moved quickly, going over to Nasima, settling between her thighs. She could barely moan before he engulfed her clit in his mouth, running his tongue back and forth over the quivering nub.

"Vino!" she screamed again and came hard, her release splashing onto his tongue. Trevino drank every drop and slurped the remnants from her pussy lips, vulva, and thighs while she whimpered and begged. When he was finally satisfied, he sat back between his two loves and pulled them over into his arms. Nasima snuggled close, still too overwhelmed to talk. Bashir stood up and left the living room, coming back a few minutes later with warm, wet cloths, bottled water, and a small bowl of strawberries. The two men put Nas between them, wiping her down and cuddling her, making sure she hydrated and replenished after so much exertion. Their Lil Baby was sensitive, and they worried constantly about pushing her body too far.

"I can't believe you just woke up and rewrote the ending like that," Butta said.

Trevino laughed. "I wasn't expecting it. Tired as I was, I should have slept right through y'all. But I'm glad I was awake for the best part."

"We didn't take care of you, Vino," Nas said drowsily, reaching over to caress his semi-hard dick through his boxer briefs. Trevino kissed her forehead.

"I'm good. Ya'll put on a hell of a show, and it was all I needed."

"We should get our lazy asses up and get in our bed, where it's more comfortable. Then we can turn the tables on Trev in the morning," Butta said. The three of them gathered themselves and turned off the TV, then headed upstairs.

The Air Between Us- The Marriage Conversation

B^{ashir} "You and Keona talking about marriage, huh?" Bashir asked Easy. The two of them, along with Romelo and Trevino were sitting in lounge chairs around the fire pit, blunts in rotation. The women were at the picnic table, covered by a huge umbrella, enjoying their dessert—grilled peaches topped with ice cream and crumbled shortbread cookies—and conversing among themselves. Easy and Keona's son, EJ, was asleep on a lounging chair in the shade. He'd eaten and run himself ragged in their spacious yard.

Their very first family event at the house was a success, and Bashir couldn't be happier. Between the perfect weather, peaceful barbecue, and knowing Nas was most likely pregnant, he was on cloud nine.

"Yeah, man," Easy replied, blowing out smoke. "I waited long enough, you know. I've known she was mine since we were seventeen years old. Life got in the way too many times already. This time, I ain't letting it."

"Y'all got the house and the kid—the bond is there. Might as well make it official," Romelo said.

"Don't use those words when you propose, though," Trevino laughed.

"Who's proposing?" Nasima asked as she and the other women walked up. They started passing out plates of dessert to the men. Trevino put out the blunt and Bashir started waving the smoke away. If anyone thought they were behaving strangely, no one said so. It made Bash wonder if there was more than one possibly pregnant woman among them.

"Easy is," Romelo said. "We were helping him figure out how to surprise Key."

"I don't want a surprise—tell me now," Keona said, and everyone laughed. She sat in her man's lap, and he leaned up to kiss her gently.

"Let me do this my way, woman. I got it," he told her. Trevino dragged over more chairs and soon, they were all sitting together. Bashir lit the fire pit, and someone put a blanket over EJ.

"You guys ever think about how you'll manage marriage, or if you want to get married? I mean, only two of you will be able to legally, so I wondered," Keona said, gesturing to the others. Romelo kissed Sadie's hand, then Bianca's.

"I'll do whatever they want to do," he said. "I don't need to get married, and I honestly haven't given it much thought."

"The truth is, I haven't either," Bianca admitted. "We're still working things out with us. I want to make sure these two know I'm not going anywhere again. That's my focus now."

"I don't think marriage is really for me, you know. Tried it right out of high school—no thanks. I'm fine with the way we are."

"Sadie, you were married before?" Nasima asked, surprised. The rest of the group, outside of Romelo and Bianca, were surprised as well.

Sadie nodded. "To the first boy who made me come. Turns out it was all he could do. Lazy in every other aspect of his life. Wanted me to 'carry' us until he could tap into his trust fund at twenty-two. I told him he had me fucked up, then I told my daddy I thought I was pregnant and agreed to the marriage under duress. Annulled in three weeks."

"My Shug doesn't stay anywhere she don't want to be," Romelo laughed. The rest of them laughed too.

"What about y'all?" Keona said, pointing at Bashir, Trevino, and Nasima.

Nasima sighed. "I want Bash and Vino to get married."

They all stared at her.

"Really? Why us?" Trevino wanted to know.

"Y'all have this great foundation, and you had it before me, you know. I think we should celebrate your finding someone so suited for you. I didn't make you guys perfect by joining you; I joined something that was perfect already," Nasima explained.

Bashir shook his head, frowning. How dare this little woman try to downplay her impact on their hearts?

"First of all, I don't want to hear you speak about yourself as if you're some afterthought. We weren't perfect. We were happy, yes. But don't ever try to lessen what you did for us."

"Butta is right. You made all this possible. We waited for you," Trevino insisted. Nasima smiled, and her eyes glistened with tears.

"Second, I think it should be you and Trev for pretty much the same reason," Bashir continued.

"You do?" Easy said.

Bashir shrugged. "Nas and Trev have a history. I mean, their love story is a lifetime in the making. If any of us are going to be married, I think it should be them."

"Bash, that's how you see us? That's so beautiful," Nasima said and burst into tears. He pulled her into his lap and held her tightly. *Our Lil Baby is definitely pregnant,* he mused.

"It is beautiful, Butta. But I'm clearly the practical one because you and Lil Baby will be the ones getting married. In fact, I think we should make it happen in the next few years."

"Why us?" Bashir said. Nasima wiped her eyes and sat up, looking at him too.

Trevino's eyebrows lifted. "If anything ever goes south for me, it's easier for the Feds to hem y'all up if you're tied to me legally.

They could come for Nas's accounts we set up for her, or the house, or your gym, Butta. If you and Nas marry each other, you're protected better than if one of you is married to me."

Bashir smiled, his heart filling with love for them. Trevino was the best at taking care of them, and things like this always proved it. He was making sure their future was secure in the only way the streets taught him how to. It was as romantic as the enforcer had ever been.

"Oh, Vino, always anticipating, aren't you?" Nasima said softly, blowing him a kiss. He grinned at her.

"You know it's what I do. It's—"

"How we survive," everyone finished for him. The group burst into laughter and went back to their conversation.

Books By Shameka S. Erby

The McNeals
The Driver's Seat
Find My Way Back
The Officer and The Butterfly
The Greatest Risk

The Royals
Hooked on Your Love
Until You Come Back To Me
All I Need
Don't Play That Song
I Never Loved A Man (Winter 2024)

The Elements Series
The Air Between Us
Her Solid Ground
His Fire and His Ice (Coming Soon)

Short Story Collections
Heartbreak Alley
Blood Ties

Acknowledgements

To **Jaleesa**- Thank you for never forgetting me
To the **Books and Shenanigans Discord**- Thank you for giving me a place for Shameka the Writer and Shameka the Reader to grow.
The Chary Assist- Thank you for all your help and support.
AK Edits- Thank you for loving on these people the way I do.
To **Kimmie Ferrell**- Your audience will find you... I did. <3